CHRIS JOHNS

Gabriel's Hope
Plantation

Gay Romance Erotica

WARNING

This book contains sexually explicit scenes and adult language. It may be considered offensive to some readers. This book is for sale to adults ONLY.

* * * * * * * * * * * * * * * * * * * *

Please store your files wisely where they cannot be accessed by underage readers.

Please feel free to send me an email. Just know that these emails are filtered by my publisher. Good news is always welcome.

Chris Johns - **chris_johns@awesomeauthors.org**

You might also want to check my blog for Updates and interesting info.
http://chris-johns.awesomeauthors.org/

About the Publisher
4Fun Publishing, a member of **BLVNP Incorporated**, 340 S. Lemon #6200, Walnut CA 91789, info@blvnp.com / legal@blvnp.com
NOTE: Due to the highly emotional reaction of some people to works of erotic fiction, any email sent to the above address that contains foul language or religious references is automatically deleted by our anti-spam software and will not be seen. All other communications are welcome.

DISCLAIMER
Please don't be stupid and kill yourself. This book is a work of FICTION. Do not try any new sexual practice that you find in this book. It is fiction and not to be confused with reality. Neither the author nor the publisher or its associates assume any responsibility for any loss, injury, death or legal consequences resulting from acting on the contents in this book. Every character in this book is over 18 years of age. The author's opinions are not to be construed as the opinions of the publisher. The material in this book is for entertainment purposes ONLY. Enjoy.

Gabriel's Hope Plantation

Gay Romance Erotica

By: Chris Johns

© Chris Johns 2014

ISBN: 978-1-62761-833-5

Chapter 1

Gabriel knew about the plantation. He was named after his grandfather, who in turn, was named after his father and his uncle who now owned the plantation. The family's lawyer had summoned him to the plantation. At 19 years old, he had never been here before and had only seen his uncle, the present owner, once in his life and that was at thirteen. Walking from town he had plenty of time to think about his life.

Sarah, his mother, had become pregnant out of wedlock. The family had cast her adrift because of the disgrace. The only concession her father had made was to purchase a small cottage for her to live in, in the nearby town. She was forbidden to have any contact with her brother, or any other member of the family. His father had been a soldier of fortune according to Sarah, when Gabriel had asked.

"I was a silly romantic girl, and your father swept me off my feet. You look very much like him, Gabriel, he was a very handsome young man."

Gabriel learnt very little more about his father than that and even less about Gabriel's Plantation. It wasn't until his uncle called on them when he was 13 that he even knew he was related to the great family.

He remembered the visit in detail. He had been playing at the front of the cottage with Joshua, his only real friend, a free black. The man who stepped down from the luxury carriage with his black driver all dressed up was a sight for sore eyes. He was very tall and his clothes probably cost more than Sarah earned in a year. He walked into the cottage as though he owned it and addressed Sarah as 'Sister.'

Gabriel stood in the doorway looking in wonder. Was this man his uncle? That couldn't be. If his uncle was very wealthy, why were he and his mother struggling to live? All was soon revealed when his uncle spoke.

"I am sure you will not grieve at the news, Sarah, but mother and father were killed in a carriage accident a week ago. I am now the master of Gabriel's Hope and as such feel I have a duty to you, my sister, and your boy. I would like you both to come to the mansion to live but my wife will not entertain that suggestion. The only thing I can do therefore is to settle an allowance on you to improve your life."

With that he looked around him. The cottage was clean, but that was all you could say about it. The furniture was old and almost beyond useful life, the drapes and rugs on the floor were thread bare and not fit, even for a slave's quarters, and both Gabriel and his mother were dressed in rags almost.

"I will instruct my bank to transfer a sum of money every month into an account for your personal use."

With that, he left, and Gabriel was left stunned at what he had just heard. Things changed for him after that. He soon had a decent set of clothes and slowly the house took on a new look. His mother spoilt him so that the first big improvement other than his clothes, was his bedroom. He had a new bed, with all new fresh linen, a proper stowage for his clothes, new drapes at the window. It was like something out of a fairy tale for Gabriel. His mother's background showed in the good taste exhibited in the cottage. By the time he started work he was well presented and lived in a nice home.

Joshua and Gabriel were the same age and because no whites wanted to associate with Sarah as a disgraced woman, Gabriel had no white friends. His mother privately tutored the children of rich families so that until he was old enough to sit in on the lessons, he spent his days with Joshua's family. His mother had insisted he get a good education, and it had paid dividends, he was now a senior accounting clerk in the offices of one of the great trading companies.

Joshua was still his only real friend, but that friendship harboured a dangerous secret. Gabriel was a boy lover and more precisely a lover of black boys, with Joshua leading the pack. Gabriel had spent many happy hours from the age of six teaching Joshua what he knew so that when he stopped schooling at sixteen and went to work, Joshua could read and write as well as do numbers. Of course it didn't help him get work because no one would employ an educated black in any work normally carried out by a white man.

'I can't remember when I first knew I loved him,' was Gabriel's thought as he walked. He remembered having weird feelings as he drove towards puberty, and those feelings became more intense after puberty. Whenever he looked at Joshua he got an erection. It was very embarrassing because being very poor, he had no underclothes and his trousers were always very thin because they were old and really, hardly wearable. Joshua's clothes were the same making his long cock very prominent as he too passed through puberty.

Gabriel's love for Joshua didn't change and as he grew. He started to outpace Joshua in growth because he was now being fed properly. The result was that as he outgrew his clothes they were passed to Josh, and he began to look smarter than some of the poor whites. Intelligent and observant, Josh realised that his good fortune was because of Gabriel's love for him. Because of that Josh allowed Gabriel more liberty with his body. Mutual hand jobs developed and at last Gabriel got one of his wishes, he was allowed to give Josh a blowjob. Much as Gabriel wanted the final action, Josh never used his cock to make Gabriel's life perfect.

At 19, Josh was still his only real friend and they still spent a lot of time together. He had wanted Josh to join him on the walk to the plantation, but had no idea what it was all about so he resisted the temptation to ask.

The day was typical of the start of the hurricane season. Very warm and cloudy, the clouds kept in the heat and increased the humidity. This next three months would be the ones Gabriel hated the most, even doing nothing one perspired. When he thought it was safe, he took his jacket and shirt off. He didn't want to turn up at the mansion looking like a puddle. Before entering the gates of the plantation, he used the tail of his shirt to wipe away as much sweat as he could, used the wet tails to calm his wild hair and passed through the very imposing portals looking mildly smart.

Standing at the front door of the mansion, Gabriel was very nervous, he rang the bell and waited. A liveried black servant answered the door and asked who he wished to see.

"I am Gabriel Sinclair and have been asked here by Mr. Balfour."

The slave immediately became very obsequious and ushered Gabriel into a luxurious entrance hall.

"Please wait here, Sir."

The servant/slave disappeared through double doors and returned very quickly.

"Mr. Balfour will see you immediately, Master." The form of address took Gabriel aback, he was no one's master.

The room he entered was like something out of a dream. It was huge, lined with bookcases all crammed full of leather bound volumes. Oh how he would have loved access to these as he grew up. Moreover, the furniture in the room was all the most beautiful he had ever seen. The most prominent piece was the desk, a huge mahogany one, inlaid with gold coloured leather and sat on two beautifully carved pedestals.

The chair was padded green leather with gold studding and large mahogany arms. Above his head were fans rotating as though by themselves, it didn't take him long after that meeting to find out how they worked. The air was still hot, but being circulated made it much more bearable.

He was directed to the desk chair. Gabriel was so nervous, not knowing what was going on that he almost wet his trousers. He sat, looked round the room again and for the first time noticed the woman sitting in the wing-backed chair facing him. She was quite beautiful, dressed in fine silk, which made Gabriel angry, and he didn't know why. The image was spoilt by the disdainful look on her face. Gabriel almost sniggered at his thought. She looked as though she had just trod in some dog shit. She was, Gabriel guessed, only a few years older than his mother.

His attention turned then to Mr. Balfour as he started to talk.

"Mr. Sinclair, your uncle Gabriel was recently killed in a hunting accident. His will only has two beneficiaries, both of whom are in this room."

He then proceeded to read the will that was, as expected, loaded with legal jargon half of which Gabriel didn't understand.

"To put it in layman's terms, Mr. Sinclair, Mrs. Sinclair, on the death of your uncle," looking at Gabriel, "Your husband," looking at the woman, "He has willed that the plantation and all its assets automatically become the property of the oldest living male of the family. Mr. Gabriel Sinclair is that person as you, Mrs. Sinclair, have no children.

The will states that unequivocally and makes only a few specific requests. Mr. Sinclair, your uncle wished you to allow your aunt to keep all the jewellery and trinkets she collected during the marriage, further, he would like her to remain in the only home she has known for the majority of her life. Failing that, he wishes you to place her in a home of her own to be purchased by you for her soul benefit."

Gabriel looked at this woman who could have made his mother's life so pleasant after the death of his grandparents but had refused to allow her that comfort. He wondered if his uncle had thought of that when he had added the clause about other suitable accommodation.

"I will think on this, Mr. Balfour, but I can assure you, Mrs. Sinclair, that you will definitely not be living here. I am sure my mother would be much kinder than I am because I know she is a wonderful, kind and loving person. My reason, I'm sure you know."

Turning to Mr. Balfour, Gabriel continued.

"Mr. Balfour, my uncle would have let my mother and I live here in comfort and luxury after the death of my grandparents. This woman vetoed it, so for another six years my mother has had to work hard to support us, and continue to live in a small cottage not befitting her position as the daughter of a wealthy plantation owner."

Once again focusing on his aunt, Gabriel spoke again, "You may, Madame, remain here until I have honoured my uncle's wish and found you a suitable accommodation."

The woman looked stunned and protested, but not for long.

"Madame, I am not required by law to follow any of my uncle's requests, and if you continue to annoy me I shall take great pleasure in throwing you out with nothing. Mr. Balfour, I know nothing about running a plantation. I presume my uncle had an estate manager and overseers for the slaves. Would you arrange for them to be called and presented to me here in half an hour? The boy that showed me in can use that time to show me round the house and introduce me to my house staff. Madame, I suggest you return to your quarters with whoever you need from the staff and start packing your possessions because I will have you moved as soon as possible. Mr. Balfour, I would also like a letter from you to the bank that will allow me to take charge of my uncle's finances."

The woman scuttled out and Gabriel was introduced to the slave that had shown him in before Mr. Balfour went to find the required people

"What's your name, Boy, and how old are you?"

Almost shaking too hard to speak, faced with his new owner, the boy stuttered out a reply. "I'm called Jess, Sir, and I'm 19 years old, as far as I can tell."

Gabriel had scoped out this boy thoroughly while they both spoke. He had an interesting bulge in the crotch of his trousers and he was similarly built to himself and Joshua.

"Well you can stop shaking, Jess, because I'm not an ogre, nor do I intend to start acting like one. You are a very attractive young man, and I know I am the master, but I hope we can be friends as well."

Poor Jess, his eyes nearly popped out of his head. To be friends with his white master, absolutely unheard of. What was this young master playing at?

Shown round the house, except for the mistress' suite, Gabriel told Jess where he would be sleeping. Alongside his designated room was a smaller room that Gabriel decided would house a bath and he would have a table in there with a washbasin on it and a jug.

He would have the door to the corridor blocked off and one opened into his bedroom to replace it, so that he had an en-suite bathroom, which was not called that in 1857 but that was what it was in reality. When he got close to Jess he realised that his smell was that of cologne.

"How often do you bathe, Jess?"

The boy looked flustered again.

"Every week, Master."

"And the remainder of the time you cover your body odour with colognes, correct?"

"Yes, Master."

"Well starting today, you are to bathe every day and you are not to use cologne at all. Also, it is much too hot to wear all that silly uniform. In future you will wear your trousers and a white shirt, your shoes as well of course, but not that jacket or all those ruffs and things, they are much too hot."

Jess wanted to sing, this was so much more than he could have wished for.

The house was marvellous and Gabriel knew his mother would know how to run it efficiently having been brought up in it. After talking to his white employees, he would take a tour of the plantation. In his study were three men, besides Mr. Balfour.

"Mr. Sinclair, this is Mr. Thomas, your estate manager; Mr. Gamble and Mr. Brown, your overseers. I'll be leaving you now, Sir, and perhaps you will call on me in chambers at your convenience to collect all the necessary paperwork."

Gabriel sat at his desk trying not to look too nervous.

"Good morning, gentlemen. I have much to do in town before I can devote my time exclusively to the plantation. Mr. Thomas, please carry on as normal. If you have any pressing need of my presence I will try to make contact with you every morning before I leave the plantation if that is my plan for the day. Mr. Gamble and Mr. Brown, I will become a hands-on owner very quickly, until then you will take your orders from Mr. Thomas, which I presume you have been doing anyway."

They touched their forelocks and left. Gabriel thought this first meeting had gone well. Next, he summoned Jess and asked him to have a carriage ready for him as soon as he had looked over his domain and a cart to bring to the house personal things from his present abode. He had

19 years of relative hardship to make up for and Gabriel didn't intend to waste any of it.

The tour of the plantation was a revelation. The fields were well tended but the slave quarters were disgusting, hardly habitable. He also noticed that the slaves were clad in rags, those that wore anything because he noticed that no one under about fourteen appeared to wear anything at all.

Some of the young teen boys looked so sexy Gabriel blushed at his own reaction.

Chapter 2

Sarah couldn't even begin to imagine what had prompted Gabriel's summons to the big house. So, she had sat at home worrying. She was quite shocked when he returned, being driven in a beautiful carriage and with another cart for goods. He jumped from the carriage, took his mother in his arms and danced her round the tiny parlour telling her of their good fortune.

"There are servants here to help you Mother. Pack everything you want to take to the big house. I am now the master of Gabriel's Hope and you are the mistress."

He explained about her brother's death and what he intended to do with his aunt.

"She condemned us to this place after your parents died. I am going to send her here with the same allowance that my uncle gave you. Let her see what her miserable rejection of you caused us to live with."

Sarah was surprised at her son's forceful attitude.

"Also, Mother, I am taking Joshua's family to live with us when I am settled. They can have one of the overseer's houses on the plantation. I will employ them all so that they can start to have a good life as well. His mother can help you in the house, his father can work with the smithy, and the children will go to school like regular children. Joshua, I will train to be my accounts clerk."

Sarah was amazed how quickly Gabriel had formulated so much.

Gabriel left his mother packing and went to find Joshua. He found him doing menial jobs for one of the town's traders.

"Stop that, Josh, go and tell your boss you are leaving. Don't make any fuss about money owed, it won't be enough to worry about. You have a new job, you are going to be the accounts clerk at Gabriel's Hope Plantation."

Joshua looked at Gabriel as though he was mad.

"I'm the new owner, Josh; my uncle died and I'm the sole surviving male."

Josh was goggle eyed, and it got even better for him.

"Your whole family is to come to the plantation to live. Mother will employ your mother in the house, I will employ your father, and the kids will be educated as well."

Josh couldn't take it all in, his best friend, his only white friend was going to be his savior. He knew he would do anything for Gabriel now. What he didn't realise was what the anything would entail.

"I'll send a cart for you tomorrow, Josh. Don't worry if it is quite late because I want the cottage all cleaned and made ready for your family first."

What Gabriel intended was that when he was finished with the carriage the next day, he was going to send that for the family and the cart for their goods.

Back at the mansion and Gabriel found his aunt still packing, but now it was anything she could lay her hands on.

"I think, Madame, I will ask a housemaid to help you unpack everything other than your clothes and your jewellery. If there is anything else that I think you should have I will forward it to you. Be ready to leave as soon as the wagon arrives from my old home. I will sign title to my old home over to you when I see Balfour tomorrow."

His aunt looked at him almost spitting venom.

"What am I to do about servants?"

"Oh I doubt there would be room for any in the cottage, and you obviously didn't think my mother should have any so I guess you will manage without as well."

In one day, by the time he and his mother sat down to dinner in the main dining room, Gabriel thought he had achieved a great deal. He had left Josh at home helping his parents pack the family's belongings.

The best part of the day for Gabriel was bathing because he had Jess bathe him, and he reciprocated. When he had his private bathroom he thought things would get even better. As it was, he had great fun. He sat back in his bed before sleeping and thought about it

He had asked Jess to have loads of hot water available and they would bath together. Jess couldn't believe this until he was by the bath and he was undressing his new master. Gabriel was very hard by the time Jess had finished and he thought his cock would burst out of his skin by the time he had Jess naked as well.

"I'm going to wash you first, Jess, so that you know how I want you to do me."

Taking much too long over the groin area, Gabriel was well satisfied with the result. Jess had a tidy cock and balls and had a very satisfying orgasm as Gabriel jacked his cock and played with his balls.

"I hope you enjoyed that Jess, because we will do it often, and maybe more."

Jess blushed before replying, "It was very exciting, Master. I liked it."

Gabriel laughed and leant forward to give Jess a light kiss on the lips.

"I think we might have lots of fun when I am truly settled in, but for now come and talk to me about the field slaves."

Gabriel wanted to hear about how the manager and overseers treated them, what punishments were handed out, how the women and girls were treated, etc. By the time he went to bed he had much to think about.

Rape of the young women by the overseers was common, beatings, for very minor offences were also quite common. Gabriel thought that was quite disgraceful and the rape was an enormous sin.

The next morning Gabriel went into town again to see Mr. Balfour. He signed all the documents and then was presented with details of his bank holdings. He was amazed, most of it was in gold bullion. What also amazed him was the quantity, how could his family have made so much off the backs of slaves when they lived in such squalor. Gold was a commodity that had permanent value but few people held it nowadays. He thought it was a good idea but he disliked banks so he started to think about what he could do with it.

Back at the plantation he sat with Mr. Thomas for a while going through the books. He said nothing, but as a senior accounts clerk he very quickly saw where Thomas, in cahoots he guessed with the overseers were skimming profits, that became even more obvious when he thought about the slave quarters and realised that nowhere near the amount of money showing in the accounts for their upkeep had actually been spent.

He rode badly, realising he would need his stableman to teach him, but he managed to stay in the saddle to view his domain again in the light of his increased knowledge. The slaves' clothes were again quite obviously not being replaced as often as the accounts would have him believe, most of the men were barely decent their trousers were so worn.

When he got back to the mansion he asked Jess to send the stableman to him immediately, and the senior work gang slaves, when they finished work.

Isaiah was the stableman and Gabriel briefed him.

"I want you to take this letter into town to the rooms of Mr. Balfour, the lawyer, can you do that for me?"

"Oh, yes, Master if you give me a pass."

"Ok, Isaiah, take a horse and go now."

When Isaiah returned he had Mr. Balfour with him, looking quite worried.

"Mr. Balfour, I'm going to sack my manager and overseers. They have been stealing quite large sums from the estate, and the slaves are the ones that have suffered. I want you to witness my words so that I can get rid of them without any compensation."

Balfour was quite shocked. "How will you run your estate without these men?

Gabriel laughed, "I'm going to do the unthinkable, I'm going to put my work gang foremen in charge and I'm going to have a black accounts clerk to monitor expenditure while I learn how to run the place."

It was comical to Gabriel to see how Balfour reacted.

"I promise you, Mr. Balfour, I will keep in touch with you even though I don't need to. I will almost certainly, as time goes by, have much need of your services. Also, I want to move my gold out of the bank. Can you suggest a safe haven for it not in any bank?"

"When you are finished with the men, Mr. Sinclair, I will show you something."

Gabriel wasn't going to risk any trouble so he briefed his work gang's leaders beforehand. They were amazed, but turned up as ordered grasping pick axe handles and stood behind Gabriel and Mr. Balfour.

"Mr. Thomas, Gamble and Brown, I don't intend to beat about the bush. I have been through the accounts thoroughly, I have cross checked expenditure with goods received and the discrepancy must have made all three of you quite wealthy men."

If Balfour and Gabriel had any doubts before, the looks passed between the three men cleared them.

"I have two choices, I can just sack you and have you clear of the estate in thirty minutes, or I can call the law and have you searched, and investigated before charging you with embezzlement. I'm going for the first option. I want you off this estate now. You will not take anything except the clothes on your back. Your ill-gotten gains you will leave in your cottages, if they are not there when I look, then I will have the law on you. If you are still on my land in thirty minutes I will have slaves strip you and send you on your way naked, now go."

They did, cursing the new master. Gabriel asked the foremen to wait in the hall. When the study was empty, Balfour went and locked the door before guiding Gabriel to the fireplace.

"Watch as I press these two points simultaneously."

There was a horse rearing up, carved in the mantelpiece at one end and, at full stretch for Mr. Balfour being only a little man, another horse facing the room in the centre of the fireplace. The two points were the noses of the horses. When pressed, a panel slid open at the other side of the fireplace, a trapdoor in the floor lifted to reveal a staircase leading down running along the back of the fire.

"The fireplace in the next room backs on to this so there is no obvious discrepancy in the shape of the walls. If the house were destroyed I still doubt this stairwell would be discovered."

At the bottom was a small room with a table and chair, and a candle in a holder on the table, which Balfour lit.

"Still nothing to see but if I put a little weight against this wall here..."

With that, Balfour stepped into a corner and pushed the wall, it swivelled revealing a larger room.

"You could store the whole of the country's gold in here."

Gabriel was amazed.

"Thank you, Mr. Balfour, I presume you are the only one besides me that knows about this."

Balfour nodded.

"I now have great cause to look after you then," and he laughed. Mr. Balfour didn't.

"Please, Mr. Balfour, I know you have served my family well and I am honoured by the way you address me, but as I am so much younger than you will you be kind enough to address me as Gabriel in the future?"

Balfour bowed a little and replied, "Thank you, Mr. Sinclair, I am honoured, but it may take me a little while to get used to that, Gabriel," now a smile crossed his face and Gabriel was pleased.

Joshua was going to be shown this at some point in the future, probably when they stowed the gold in here. The secret was all hidden again and it was time to move on.

"Isaiah, ride back to town with Mr. Balfour and take a spare horse. I want you to bring my friend Joshua with you and make sure his family has all the help they need to pack up and come to the estate."

Addressing the foremen that were waiting in the entrance hall Gabriel said,"Foremen, go and handle your crews. Don't let me down or I'll bring in new overseers."

Balfour went, wondering at the energy this new young master was exhibiting. When Josh arrived, Gabriel couldn't resist temptation. He took him in his arms and kissed him on the lips. Before he could react he spoke.

"We are going to have so much fun running this plantation, Josh, and we are going to start now."

Gabriel explained what he was going to do.

"I'm going to let the gang foremen run the gangs with no white overseers. I'll get you to issue the orders for anything we need to buy, and you just bring them to me each day for my signature. I'm going to show you how I want the books kept. Jess is presently a houseboy, but I think we can use him as our errand and messenger boy. All three of us are going to learn how to ride. I'm not going to let you and Jess waste time walking everywhere, which is counterproductive."

In the three years since leaving school, Gabriel had watched, listened, and learnt. So much money was wasted following old ways in business, he wasn't going to have that.

The gang foremen came to the house to report at the end of the day, and Gabriel sat them on the back porch and had a large jug of cool lemonade ready for them.

"Now, who is the senior man here?"

They all looked at a man mountain about 30 years old.

"I guess I am, Master; I'm Ezekiel."

Gabriel laughed, "Well you are now Zeke, I could waste days saying all of your names."

The men laughed.

"I want you to give me the name of another man who could be a gang foreman."

The man chosen was Abraham who would become Abe. Jess was sent to get him.

"Zeke, this is my proposal. Each gang surrenders two men to me and they will work with Abe. Provided you can promise me that the depleted gangs will get as much work done as they do now I will use this new gang to start building new cabins for families to live in. Your families, your women, and your children should be together, and I want that to happen. The old cabins we will pull down as they empty, they are too far decayed to even think about wasting more money on. I also want you to send me as many of the women as you can that are seamstresses. Starting with the ladies we are going to see some pretty dresses around here, then we'll think about putting some not so pretty dresses on you men." Another laugh and exchanged looks wondering at this new master.

"I'm not crazy, but the expenditure on these things has been going into the overseers pockets, now it's going to you. Any problems with that, Zeke, and the rest of you?"

Much shaking of heads.

"Zeke, you have Abe and his work gang wait at the cottages in the morning, Josh and I will be there to start the ball rolling on this. Remember, don't let me down or I'll bring in new overseers. Report to me at the end of work each day."

He went down to the overseers and managers' cottages and collected piles of dollars. He was sure they would still have left with plenty, but this haul would build a lot of cottages.

Gabriel told his mother what he had ordered.

"Please, Mother, take a cart and the carriage, go into town tomorrow and buy loads of pretty material. Let our women start to look good for their men."

After dinner that night, having checked that Josh's family were moved in and settling, Gabriel asked Josh to sleep with him.

"We have so much to do, Josh, it would be good to be able to talk in bed as well."

Josh wasn't stupid. "Will that be in between kisses and whatever else you have planned?"

He was grinning and Gabriel was as well, before getting very serious.

"I've never felt I could say this before, Josh, but now I can. I love you, more than a brother. I think I've always loved you, but after puberty I knew it was a special kind of love, forbidden in our society."

Josh, looking serious replied. "I know, I think I've known for a long time. I don't know for sure how I feel. I know I love you as well, but I don't know how far I can go with this boy/boy sex."

"We'll worry about it as we go along then shall we, but can I kiss you goodnight?"

Josh laughed, "Yes, Gabriel, I think I'd like that."

Cuddling Joshua that night, both of them naked, was something Gabriel had dreamt about, without realistically believing it would ever happen. Now it was and it was heaven. Josh could feel the tears falling on his back, but he knew they were happy tears so he said nothing. He could also feel a very hard cock pressed into the crack of his ass that didn't worry him either.

The sex thing would work itself out but Josh was sure he would do anything Gabriel wanted, he owed him so much already and it was set to get better.

Chapter 3

The next day was another involving manic activity.

Josh's mother, Oprah, came to work with Gabriel's mother; his father Landon went to work with the blacksmith and the small children joined the slave children to play while Gabriel sorted education.

Josh and Gabriel went into the slave cottages to talk to Abe. Working together they sorted out the location for the new cottages for families.

"Don't go over the top, Abe, but make the cottages big enough for an average family to live comfortably. Work out how much timber you need for two, to start with, and give your order to Josh."

Josh broke in then.

"Perhaps I'd better stay, Gabriel. I don't suppose any of these men write."

Gabriel blushed. "I'm sorry, I never thought. Ok, Josh, I'll manage without you for the morning. Lunch with me and then after lunch we are taking horse riding lessons."

The day turned out to be tiring, but satisfying. The final bit was the meeting with his work supervisors who reported their progress.

"I'm just starting to learn this business, Zeke, so you could bullshit me easily. I won't know for sure until after the harvest has been sold. If it is down on last year's figures I'll go into reverse on trusting you and bring in a white manager and overseers, and I won't restrict what they do to get results."

The message was loud and clear. There would be no more rapes of their women, or punishment beatings provided they didn't let the master down. What they didn't know yet was that some of the young men would be gracing the master's bed on occasions.

End of day two and the happiness on Gabriel's Hope was breaking out all over.

Water was not an issue with a substantial stream running through the property. The problem as far as Gabriel could assess it was that it would take a lot of man power, or more precisely, woman power, to bring sufficient quantities to the house and slave village for his thoughts on hygiene to be realised.

A few days later after a trip to town to talk to some metal workers the problem was potentially solved. A lifting pump would be made, capable of pumping water from the river to storage tanks he would have made and fitted at the village and the house. It took time but a month after taking over he had what he wanted. The village was dominated by a water tower and one was constructed close to the house as well. Several strong men were allocated part time to pump water up to the tanks through a series of pipes.

In a similar time scale many new cottages had been built for families and larger barrack type cottages for the single men and women. Zeke had quickly assumed the role of senior overseer and was on excellent terms with Gabriel.

"Zeke, I don't know how the old master handled the mating of the women, but this is my law. No buck will have sex with a girl without my consent. Break that rule and get a girl pregnant and I'll strip the hide from the back of the buck. Where possible I will allow young couples to marry and set up home in a new cottage, but that is it. I want to see all men as they reach eighteen when I will assess them and decide how and where they will work. I still have to think about a good breeding programme to keep the plantation at work in the future."

Assessing the young men at eighteen was a nice way of saying, I'm going to check out future bed partners, or more precisely sex partners. Josh was being very co-operative with man/man sex, but Gabriel wanted to be the top and Josh wasn't happy with the idea of a cock up his ass. He had bowed to Gabriel's desire to be fucked, but more on that later. To get to this point after only one month had taken a huge amount of work on everyone's part.

Sarah had the running of the house sorted very quickly, she had also put seamstresses to work making dresses for the women and eventually new clothes for the men. They wore their old one in the fields but in the evenings, Gabriel was so happy to see them congregating in the centre of the village to sing and dance, all looking smarter and happier than they had done when he arrived. Zeke and his co-foremen were working the crews so hard that Gabriel kept Abe and his eight men on permanent maintenance on the plantation. The stableman very quickly got Gabriel, Joshua and Jess to a good standard riding.

Joshua didn't sleep with Gabriel every night, he laughed when he told him.

"I sleep with you as a special treat, Gabriel, but I think you need to empty your balls into another boy quite often."

They had laughed and Gabriel knew he had the best of both worlds. The love for Joshua was deep and his greatest joy was feeling Josh enter him on the nights they slept together. He sat back and thought about that first time, just a few days after moving in to the mansion. He had planned it well, getting some refined animal fat from the kitchen to lubricate his anus and Josh's cock.

"Josh, I want you to fuck me tonight. We can pleasure each other and you can open up my anus before trying to put your cock there."

Josh knew it was coming and didn't object, after all, look what his family had now compared with just one week ago.

Bathed and smelling sweet, the two young men piled into bed and with Joshua on his back, Gabriel started to kiss him.

"I love you so much, Josh, I will never ask you to take my cock in your arse, but if you ask for it know that it will bring me more joy than I have any right to expect."

Both boys laughed at that and Gabriel started moving down Josh's body with his kisses. His tears of happiness left a trail and Josh wondered at his luck. He did genuinely love Gabriel and he was sad that boy/ boy sex was something he had reservations about. Gabriel thrilled him as he started to attack his groin, no reservation on the enjoyment level there. His long cock got even longer as he felt the warm wet tongue lick it and his balls and then swallow the head and send him into space with the sensitivity of the tongue working his glans. Despite the size of Josh's balls, Gabriel still managed to get them both in his mouth and drive Josh crazy as his tongue worked them over.

"Oh, God, Gabriel, that is driving me crazy."

"You had better start opening me up then, Josh, because I want you to come in my arse."

For the first time, Josh took Gabriel in his mouth as he started to finger him. Gabriel was in heaven, this was more than he expected from his best friend. When he could feel four of Josh's fingers in his anus, Gabriel knew it was time.

"Now, Josh, lube my arse and your cock. Fuck me, I want this more than anything else in the world, apart from me in you."

"I'm sure I'll hurt you, Gabriel, I don't want to do this."

"I know, Josh, but please for me."

Josh was very reticent as he positioned between Gabriel's legs, but he could see the lust and the love so he pushed. His head disappeared inside his friend and he stopped still as Gabriel screamed.

"Oh, God, Josh that hurts, but don't move."

The pain took some time to abate, but when it did, Gabriel smiled and whispered, "More, Josh, feed it all to me slowly."

Josh couldn't believe how sensuous it felt on his cock as the soft tissue of Gabriel's anus gripped him, and Gabriel used his muscles to massage it.

"Oh, Gabriel, that feels amazing. After you have done it you won't want to waste time being the bottom, you'll be fucking every young buck on the plantation."

They both laughed, but the fucking was so incredible they were soon lost in the sensuality of it until they orgasmed and everyone in the house must have heard the screams of pleasure from both of them. They calmed down slowly in each other's arms and Josh's words set the tone for years of joint pleasure.

"I love you, Gabriel, and I'll do that as often as you want, but know I want to marry and have children."

Gabriel kissed his soul mate hard, and replied.

"And I want to build you a house for your family and be a special uncle to your children."

Gabriel could not have been happier, well maybe a little, if he could have fucked Josh, but he would never force the issue even though he knew he could. His love for this black man would never be stronger than it was that night.

Jess became the recipient of and centre of Gabriel's sex life for the next month, and to start with, accepted a cock in his arse reluctantly. He knew he had no choice and in all other respects the master was a marvellous person to work for, it really was a lot like having a friend. The reluctance disappeared the first time Gabriel let Jess fuck him.

"You are being such a terrific lover, Jess, would you like to fuck me tonight?"

He could barely splutter a 'yes', but when he did Gabriel laughed took him in his arms and kissed him.

"Well, go ahead, I have done it to you often enough for you to know how."

There was no problem with Jess, he was smaller than Joshua. The result was a very happy slave and a contented master. So contented that for the first time Gabriel allowed Jess to stay all night, not just for the sex. The next morning Gabriel asked for Jess' recommendation.

"Jess you are working for Joshua and me so much you really don't have time to be the butler here, who would you recommend taking your place? I need someone to meet and greet visitors when we are doing other things and help mother run the house."

Jess laughed and replied, "I know one boy, Master, I'm sure you would like him. He has an enormous cock."

Gabriel looked at Jess and then laughed.

"If you get cheeky I might use him to fuck you as well."

Jess wasn't sure if Gabriel was serious until he found himself wrapped in his arms receiving a very serious kiss.

"You had better send him to me after breakfast then, Jess, and then you can join Joshua for the morning."

Blaine was the young man Jess recommended and when he entered the study, Gabriel was pleased, he looked smart and he smelt fresh. He expected the slaves to have a musk about them but he didn't like it to be too strong.

"I am looking for a man to become the major domo in my house, do you think you could do the job?"

Blaine looked shocked.

"I'm only a field hand, Master, but I sure would like to try."

"How old are you, Blaine?"

"I'm 22, Master."

"Very good, one of your duties will be to keep me happy, sometimes in my bed. Do you think you could handle that?"

Blaine had heard the stories about the master and Joshua, and the master and other young slaves like Jess.

"It ain't my thing, I don't think, Master, but I would sure try hard to please you in any way that I can."

"In that case, provided I like what I see when you shuck down for me I'll get Jess to start training you, and my mother will measure you for your new uniform."

What he saw when Blaine stood naked before him made Gabriel's eyes water. Blaine had the biggest cock he had ever seen. It must have been longer than 12 inches soft, and it was also thicker than Joshua with an erection.

Gabriel couldn't resist it, he walked up to Blaine and started playing with it. When it was erect Gabriel's jaw hung open. It was the most awesome piece of man meat he had ever seen.

"If I can ever get that in my arse, Blaine, I may never want you to take it out again."

Blaine was completely lost now, he had no idea the master wanted to take it, he thought it was he that would have the master's cock in his arse.

"Go to see my mother now and tell her you need uniforms to take over from Jess, then find Jess and tell him to train you when he has time. Do a good job, Blaine, and you'll have a much easier life than the field hands.

Gabriel knew that without any doubt he was going to spend many an evening playing with, and sucking on that enormous appendage. He loved all the things about gay sex but his favourite was without doubt sucking on a great cock and Blaine had that in abundance.

Meeting other plantation owners and milking them for knowledge very quickly brought Gabriel up to speed in managing the plantation. He knew that Zeke was doing a good job as senior overseer and the boys worked hard for him, because they knew that they were being looked after properly, their families as well.

It was against the law to educate slaves but it wasn't against the law to show them how things worked and how to maintain them. From an early age, Gabriel had small boys watching and learning from carpenters and builders, blacksmiths and repair men. The stableman had lots of little helpers as well. Many of these boys would end up working in the fields, but they would still have other skills.

The biggest change for the slaves came after the harvest. The fields were cleared ready for replanting and then Gabriel told Zeke they were going to build a dam on the river to make a swimming hole. He had already noted the perfect place for it. There was a green glade near it and it was downstream from the pump for the accommodation areas, so he could organise swimming parties for the slaves at different times.

The sound of axes rang out around the plantation and Gabriel soon had a very good dam that gave a fine swimming hole once it was full, and then the flow to the plantation fields resumed unabated. Gabriel watched some of the work delighting in the nudity of the men as they worked in the water. Some of them were stunning to Gabriel and he knew he would be trying them in his bed at some time. A side benefit was that Gabriel had some more cleared land, and for this he decided to start a vegetable garden so that he could feed the whole plantation as well. Once it was dug, the women could look after that so he would need no new manpower.

"Zeke, I'm going to ask my mother and some of the ladies to organise a picnic for the families at the swim hole. On the same day I'm going to organise a party for the single men and women on the lawns of the big house. Do you think they would all like that?"

Zeke was dumbfounded, he had never heard of such a thing. It happened, and from that party he knew there would be some more slave marriages, meaning more cottages. He would have to be careful that this didn't get out of hand. The harvest was sold, Joshua completed the financial books for the year and was delighted to show Gabriel the accounts.

"You've done it, Gabriel, you've made more money this year than your uncle ever did."

"Thank you, Josh, we've had quite a year haven't we?"

Chapter 4

Gabriel was in town one day and at a local tavern he heard about a woman who had been thrown out of all the places she had worked because she was an abolitionist. She was a child's governess and that sparked interest in Gabriel. He sought her out and asked if she would come to the plantation with him to discuss a position.

On the ride back she pounded Gabriel's ears about the evils of slavery making Gabriel laugh. She couldn't understand why.

"Miss Hathaway, please keep your ranting to yourself until we have talked, or I might end up throwing you out of this carriage. I understand that you are now effectively destitute so I am sure the job I am thinking of offering you has a double benefit, the chance to help a large number of blacks, and a roof over your head."

She shut up. Sitting in Gabriel's study, the first thing she noticed was how relaxed and friendly the atmosphere was.

"Blaine, be so kind as to ask Molly to bring some refreshments for myself and Miss Hathaway."

The slave looked relaxed and was dressed casually instead of the silly overdressed staff that she saw in other great houses. They were just settling down when the study doors burst open and three little black urchins burst in and the eldest jumped into Gabriel's lap and gushed out.

"Is the lady going to be our new teacher, Gabe?"

Gabriel laughed and pulled the two smallest onto his lap as well.

"If you are very good, and if I am very persuasive she might be. Now why don't you go to her and introduce yourselves. Tell the lady your name and how old you are."

Ann Hathaway noted that they were clean and clothed properly.

"I'm called Jason and I'm seven."

"I'm called Missy and I'm five."

"I'm called Matthew and I'm five as well, but I'm the eldest." He looked at Gabriel who nodded, and Matthew continued. "By five minutes."

Gabriel could hardly speak he was laughing so hard, "And if you come to work here Miss Hathaway, don't ever forget that. Now, you three, off you go. Say hello to Miss Sarah and tell her I said you could have some short cake."

Squeals of delight and they were gone.

"I don't understand, Mr. Sinclair, you allow slave children to treat you like one of their own and you dress them decently."

"Well, Miss Hathaway, those three are more like my brothers and sister, and they aren't slaves. Their elder brother is my lifetime best friend and my accounts clerk here on the plantation, their mother is the senior housekeeper and my mother's friend, their father works for my blacksmith and is the closest I've ever had to a real father. Also, they are all free. Yes I have slaves, but any of them will tell you they are treated like family or workers. I pay my freemen the rate for the job, and my slaves I make sure live a good life as well. I employ no white overseers and my mother and I are the only whites on this plantation. I know your political leanings, but if you have a look at my slave village I hope you will realise I am doing better for my slaves than they could expect as free men. Since I came here no slave has been beaten, and in all truth, none of them have deserved it anyway."

That little speech finished and there was a tap on the door. A pretty young woman dressed in a fresh brightly coloured dress walked in with a tray of refreshments and lemonade.

"Miss Sarah said to pile the plate high with cookies, Mr. Gabriel, because she didn't think there would be any left by the time Jason had fed the whole village."

They both laughed and Gabriel thanked Molly.

"Your staff treat you more like an equal than the master of this plantation, Mr. Sinclair."

"Well, we are almost. We all have to work hard to enjoy the pleasure of this place."

Another interruption then as Joshua entered. Ann saw a young black man similar in build to Gabriel dressed casually in a white shirt and black trousers with soft deerskin boots on.

"Oh, sorry Gabriel, I didn't know you had company."

Gabriel laughed and replied. "You had better keep your brother with you then. He knew Miss Hathaway was a schoolteacher within about two minutes of us arriving here. Miss Hathaway, this is Joshua Lake, my best friend, partner in crime and bookkeeper for Gabriel's Hope, also the brother of the three urchins that have just left."

"Josh, if Miss Hathaway and I can overcome a few hurdles, she will be teaching the children."

Miss Hathaway was startled by the look of love that passed between the two men.

"You didn't need to do that, Gabriel, you have already done so much for my family."

"Josh, you are worth it. Now what was it you wanted?"

"Sorry, I need these acquisitions signed. Abe and his gang have run out of timber and the carpenter needs some more for furniture for the new cottages. I'm sorry, Gabriel, our own sawmill can't keep up with demand. The timber bill this month is going to be quite large."

Gabriel shrugged, signed them without checking them and said, "We have to make up for the lack of investment in the village because of those crooks I sacked. I doubt it will bankrupt us, Josh," and Joshua left.

"Do you never check his work, Mr. Sinclair?"

"Of course I do, when we go through the accounts each week. I'm afraid timber is eating up a lot of money at the moment, but I promised my overseers that I would house families together and for that we need a lot more cottages."

Ann Hathaway found this man difficult to fathom. He was a slave owning plantation owner, but treated his staff like free men.

"Please, let's have a drink and then come with me, I'm sure a lot of your questions concerning this plantation will be answered then."

Ann spent the next hour mouth agape. The slave village was like nothing she had seen before. The first surprise was the tower with the huge tub on top.

"What's that, Mr. Sinclair?"

"Oh, that's our new water tower. We pump water from the river to this tower and the one for the house so that there is always plenty of water for the people to bathe every day after they finish work. We have a village shop where they can get essentials like soap and their food is issued from there as well. My mother, along with Joshua's mother handle clothing, but any seamstresses can ask mother for cloth and make their own clothes and the children's. I encourage the men to keep a clean set for socialising in the evenings and on Sunday when we don't work. I have dammed the creek so that we have a swim hole and the families use that extensively on Sundays. We usually have a party on the lawns for the young men and women on the same day."

"You appear to treat your slaves like free men."

"Not quite, I don't pay them."

Back in the study, Gabriel put forward his proposal.

"It's against the law to teach slaves to read and write. But, I would like you to teach the three children you have met, because they are free men. I don't think it is against the law for slave children to listen to what you say, and I'm sure we could find lots of slate and chalk for them to play with while they listen to you. I don't put the men to field work until they are sixteen, but up to that age they understudy artisans, they could also watch some of your lessons where appropriate. I know that having more workers that can read and write would make this plantation even more efficient and allow more luxuries for the workers. You and I can't achieve that legally, but we can bend the law a little if you would like the job. There is a cottage available for you and I can find one of the women that would look after you."

Ann didn't know what to say, and they hadn't even discussed a salary.

"One last thing before you make a decision. I won't tolerate any abolitionist talk on this plantation. My slaves are better treated than freed blacks are so I don't want their minds working on being worse off than they are now. Slavery can't last forever, I can see that, and when it is legal to free all my slaves I will do so, but I'm not going to agitate that prematurely." Ann, reluctantly had to agree with Gabriel and accepted the position.

"I'll send you back to town in a carriage and you can collect your things. Come back to the house and ask for Jess, I'll make sure he takes you to your cottage which is ready for occupancy."

"Thank you, Mr. Sinclair," and she was gone.

Gabriel was feeling pleased with himself. Most governesses would not have entertained the idea of teaching Negroes, free or not, so Ann was a major find.

This must have been his day for unscheduled visitors. Gabriel was using horses more and needed a young buck to help his stableman. The word had gone out that he was looking for one and a local slave agent called without an appointment.

Blaine showed him in.

"Mr. Sinclair, please accept my apology calling unannounced, but I have a young man who I think fits your requirements, and he won't be available for long when other owners know his experience. He is an excellent horseman and has been trained as a farrier. I could send him to auction but I'm not asking an unreasonable price for him so you can buy him direct if he suits you."

"Well, bring him in then, Mr. Symes, let's have a look at him."

"Here in the house, Sir?"

"Yes, Mr. Symes, I haven't time to go wandering."

Symes left and was back in a few minutes trailed by a boy, probably 20 years old. Well put together and very attractive to look at.

"Shuck down boy and let me have a look at you."

The boy did and Gabriel felt a tingle in his groin. He walked up to the boy and stroked him, made him bend and spread his legs before licking a finger and just easing it over his sphincter. The boy didn't move. Stood again and Gabriel took hold of his cock and balls, played with them for a minute and watched the cock come to an erection. At the same time Gabriel's did as well.

'Oh, God, I hope the boy is good at his job, I want him in my bed' was Gabriel's thought.

"He looks healthy enough, Mr, Sykes, could be a good stud for breeding. What's his name and his history?"

Sykes blushed. "His name is Fernando, Sir. He is being sold because he is no good as a breeder, he only gets erections for other boys."

Gabriel had never heard of a black that was like him and he could hardly cover his joy.

"Well, Fernando, you'd better get dressed and show me that you love horses as well as boys."

Sykes was amazed and both were pleased.

At the stables, Gabriel told Isaiah that this boy was to have a freehand with the horses for half an hour. He watched as the boy checked all over the horses in the paddock not making them nervous, the reverse in fact, they were all calmer when he was inspecting them than they were normally. Gabriel listened to him as he talked gently to them. They were like putty in his hands.

"What do you think, Isaiah?"

"The boy is a natural, Sir. I know there are four shoes to be replaced, let's see if he picks them up."

Fernando came back to the three men and spoke to Gabriel.

"Four shoes need replacing, Master, and the brown mare is pregnant."

Gabriel was amazed, "Did you know that Isaiah?"

Isaiah looked embarrassed, "No, Sir, I'm sorry"

Gabriel put an arm around the older man's shoulder, "Don't worry about it, I'm sure you would have found out soon. Would you like Fernando to come and work for you?"

"Yes, Mr. Gabriel, I think I would."

"Good, take him down to the village, bath him and get him new clothes from the store, find him a bed in the bachelor house and then bring him back to the house for me. If Mr. Sykes and I have reached a satisfactory conclusion to our business he'll be yours, if not, well, we'll just have to keep looking."

Mr. Sykes had heard that the new owner of Gabriel's Hope was liberal with his treatment of slaves but seeing him treat the stableman so easily really surprised him. The surprise increased when they entered the main house again and Gabriel took the shoulder of his major domo and said.

"You'll need to keep an eye on our new farrier, Blaine, when he sees what you are packing he'll want to be between your legs all day."

Master and slave laughed conspiratorially before once again the study became the centre of their world.

"I don't want to get into a barter with you, Mr. Sykes, just give me your bottom line and I'll tell you if I want it. I don't suppose many owners will be interested in a stud that isn't."

"No, Mr. Sinclair, I'll have difficulty shifting him as anything other than a field hand I expect, farriers aren't in much demand at the moment. I would be happy at $500 more than a field hand, Sir, considering his skills."

"I think that is fair, Mr. Sykes. I can pay you that in cash now if you have the paperwork."

Business concluded and Sykes felt he had to say something more.

"You're very young to be a plantation owner, Mr. Sinclair, but it has been a pleasure to do business with a gentleman. If you ever need my services again, Sir, I will be delighted to help if I can."

Gabriel was pleased, he might well call on that word sometime.

Sykes got up to leave as the door opened and Blaine brought Fernando in.

"Show Mr. Sykes out, Blaine, and I'll call you when I want you to collect Fernando."

Fernando looked a little nervous.

"Relax, boy, you and I are going to have lots of fun when you aren't working, starting now. I want you to shuck down again and sit in that chair."

Fernando did, but he nearly passed out with shock when Gabriel undressed as well and dropped down between the boy's legs, took his cock in his mouth and gave him a fantastic blowjob. The cock wasn't incredibly long but it was thick, and what Gabriel wanted most was a boy that loved to be fucked.

"Did you enjoy that, Fernando?"

"Oh yes, Master."

"Good, would you like to do that to me now?"

A nod of the head and they reversed positions. Gabriel was delighted the boy was very good.

"If I wanted to fill your other end with my cock, what would you say?"

"Yes please, Master, I love cock in either end," and then he grinned.

"That's marvellous, Fernando. After supper tonight I want you to come to the house and ask for Blaine, he will show you to my bedroom. You are to bath thoroughly again making very sure your groin and anus are clean, I want my tongue to enjoy them."

Fernando almost bounced out of the house, and Gabriel went about his work with a huge anticipatory grin on his face.

Chapter 5

Dinner was nearly always quite informal if they had no guest, and it was not unusual for Joshua's family to eat with them. On this particular evening it was just Joshua and Miss Hathaway.

"Miss Hathaway, you have already seen we are quite informal here. I would like it therefore if you adopted first names for all the freemen. My mother is Sarah, Joshua's mother is Oprah, and his father you'll find in the blacksmith's shop working under our smithy, his name is Landon. The children you already know and I am happy to answer to Gabriel."

"Thank you, Mr. Sinclair. That may take some getting used to but I'll try. I would be delighted to be called Ann."

All smiles and the conversation became very relaxed.

"I engaged a new farrier today, Josh. He looks as though he's going to be very good, knows his horses. He's not much older than us. I got him for a good price because he's a boy lover so no good as a stud."

Josh laughed and couldn't help giving the game away.

"So I suppose I'm sleeping at home tonight."

"Well yes, that might be a good idea, although you are very welcome to stay as well."

More laughter and Gabriel changed the conversation.

"Ann, I've talked to my mother and she thinks it would be nice if you ate with us, but if you wish you can eat in your own house, the girl can cook and will be at your disposal all the time."

"Thank you, Gabriel, she is already proving very capable."

"She's the daughter of my senior overseer. Oh, Josh, the paperwork for Fernando is on my desk and tomorrow morning I think it would be a good idea for you to sit down with Ann and discuss a salary for her. I'm going to work with Zeke all day tomorrow."

"If 9 o'clock in the morning is okay, Ann, we'll meet in the study and afterwards I'll take you down to the village to the school house and you can settle in. I'll also brief Abe, our village overseer. He will make sure all the boys and girls are gathered out the front to watch. The three urchins will be there tomorrow as well."

"Huh, it looks like I could sell off all the under 16 and save myself a load of money, they aren't going to be very productive sitting on their butts outside the schoolhouse every morning."

Ann looked shocked until she saw the grin pass between Josh and Gabriel.

"Did you enjoy being Joshua's school teacher, Gabriel?"

"Oh yes, that was a labour of love for eleven years. He has always been my best friend."

Once again Ann saw the look of love pass between the two men and it dawned on her that there would be no new mistress of Gabriel's Hope, Sarah had the job for life. This was a situation she had never come across. She had heard about men that loved men, but never seen any that she knew of. These two looked so manly, how could they do things to each other of a sexual nature. The only thing to do was watch and learn, she certainly had nowhere else to go in this area.

Ann's life became a game of two halves. Teaching, which she loved, and being able to teach black children was the icing on the cake. The other half was Gabriel-watching. She realised he was very promiscuous, bedding many different young slaves, but keeping a special place for Joshua.

The amazing thing was that she saw no resentment from the young men, being used for something alien to most of their natures. Of course, the reason was that they were all aware of how badly most slaves were treated by their owners in comparison to Gabriel's treatment of them. So, a cock in their ass or their mouth wasn't what they would take by choice, but it didn't happen very often, and Gabriel was always gentle and considerate.

Female slaves were not really terribly productive, but Gabriel loathed to sell any that had family. It was Josh who gave Gabriel an idea to work on.

"Some of the gentle women in town can't afford to buy a slave, Gabriel, but they could afford to pay a small amount to keep one. Why not offer some of the teenage girls as maids to these ladies for a monthly fee, allowing them to remain in the area to see their families?"

Gabriel thought about it, talked to his mother and Oprah about it and eventually started a training programme to get the young ladies to a competent standard for maid service. It worked. Mr. Balfour drew up contracts and Gabriel advertised the service.

Sarah took charge of the placements and surprised everyone when she insisted that the girls had one day off per week, Sundays, so that they could socialise with family. Gabriel arranged a cart to fetch them all from a joint meeting point and it was a happy singing bunch of young women who returned to the plantation every Saturday night and departed again quite late Sunday nights having spent the day with family or their beau.

The scheme was so successful that the second year profits were even better than year one.

Josh was surprised at the end of that second year when Gabriel told him he was going to drive the cart into the bank.

"Before that though Josh, you are going to learn to use a firearm."

None the wiser, because Gabriel wouldn't disclose the reason why. Both men practised loading, firing and reloading pistols until they were very proficient. They also learnt how to use a sword adequately.

When all was ready, Josh found himself at the reins of the cart, double harnessed with the strongest of the work horses. At the bank there were four mounted law officers. All of Gabriel's gold was loaded into the cart and they set off for the plantation. While they were still some distance from home Isaiah and Jess rode up sporting pistols in their belts. Gabriel dismissed the law officers with his thanks and a fat bonus, to keep their mouths shut. The small party continued to the plantation and the boxes were unloaded into the study. When Josh and Gabriel were alone Gabriel locked the door and explained.

"I don't trust banks, Josh, so we are going to keep the majority of Gabriel's Hope's money here."

He showed Josh the secret partition and the basement room. Josh was amazed when the second room was revealed. They stowed all of the gold in it and closed the partition, the empty gold boxes were left in the first room.

"Can you see anything that would give the second room away?"

Josh inspected the floor and the walls in minute detail.

"That's amazing, Gabriel, I know where it is but I can't see a thing."

"If this room is ever found, they will think I have moved the gold somewhere else, just leaving the boxes. Only Mr. Balfour and us two know of this, Josh. This is our rainy day money if we ever hit on bad times.

End of the year and most of the young men were no longer gracing Gabriel's bed. He had Blaine to thrill with the huge cock, which he had learnt to take in his butt. Jess when he wanted to gently fuck someone. Josh as always for the most exciting sex with someone he continued to love deeply, but it was Fernando that graced his bed the most often. The young man was the black equivalent of Gabriel when it came to sex. He loved to fuck, but he loved Gabriel to fuck him even more.

The only tiny cloud on Gabriel's horizon was his almost overpowering desire to make love to Joshua completely. He knew he could, anytime he wanted, but he had promised Josh that he would only fuck him on request.

End of the third year and it was obvious that Matthew, at eight years old, was outstripping all other children in his absorption of knowledge. Gabriel called a family conference.

Landon and Oprah, Sarah and Ann, Josh and Gabriel.

"I've called this conference because I believe we need to do something about Matthew's schooling, and I don't know what. Ann, tell us about his abilities."

"Matthew is at the same educational level as a twelve year old white student. I believe he will be ready to go to college anywhere in the States in three more years if he continues to absorb knowledge at his present rate."

Everyone's jaws were hanging open.

"There is nowhere in the South that my brother can go to college and Ann has admitted he is outstripping her ability to teach him. The only solution I can see is to send him North to continue his education, but I have no idea where, and more importantly, whether you all think that is the correct decision."

Josh was the first to speak.

"Gabriel, if you do things your way it will cost a huge amount of money. You have already raised the living standards of this family beyond anything we could ever have expected, to do this on top would be more than I feel we deserve."

Gabriel walked round the table and to the surprise of everyone else, kissed Joshua quite passionately on the lips before returning to his seat.

"Apart from my mother, Josh, you are the dearest person in my world. There is nothing I wouldn't do to please you. Landon is the only father I have ever known, and Oprah is like a second mother to me. Your three siblings have brought me nothing but joy in the three years we have lived here. Now tell me what price you can put on that."

No one could say anything for ages and then Sarah spoke.

"Let's take this one step at a time, Gabriel. Landon and Oprah, are you prepared to let Matthew leave home to go north for his education?"

Oprah looked at Landon and the tears came to her eyes.

"There probably isn't another black in the South who will have an opportunity like this Landon. I don't want to lose him, but Gabriel's offer is mighty difficult to turn down."

"I agree with what Joshua has said, Gabriel, and with what my wife says. I trust you, Son, to make a decision that is best for the family but more than anything protects Matthew."

"Ann, any ideas for a school for Matthew?"

"Yes, Gabriel. There is a school in Boston that caters for exceptionally gifted students. I wasn't qualified enough to gain a position when I applied. It is mixed race and all ages. It's also very expensive, but they say tomorrow's leaders will come from there."

"If I purchase a house close to the school, would you be prepared to go with Matthew and look after him?"

Ann was torn now, of course she would, Matthew was her prize student and they got on so well.

"I would love to, Gabriel, but what about the school here?"

"Matthew will need you more than the school will and I promise to do everything in my power to replace you. My mother, Joshua and myself will try to devote sometime to teaching while we find a new teacher. I'll travel to Boston and make all the arrangements and I'll send staff from here to run the house. Their gift will be their freedom."

Joshua had become a good bean counter and he was totalling up the costs as Gabriel spoke.

"Gabriel, even without the school fees the cost is astronomical."

"Josh, how much has my fortune increased since I came here?"

"Too much to mouth at this table, Gabriel."

"Earned by a hundred black slaves. Now I can repay them for their hard work by sending a boy of colour to take on the world. I'd do it for a slave as well if we find one as clever as Matthew."

That appeared to be settled. Gabriel would leave Joshua to run the plantation and advertise for a new teacher, black or white. He and Ann would head for Boston to organise everything, with Matthew in tow.

Double first class compartments was the only way Matthew could travel with them so the rail trip to Boston was carried out in luxury with Matthew virtually glued to the window all the way during daylight hours and he slept snuggled up to Gabriel every night.

Gabriel and Ann were at their most persuasive with the principal of the school, but after Mathew's test results were seen they needn't have bothered.

"The boy is amazing, and you say he has only been in education for three years?"

Ann nodded and explained how.

"He is too young to board, but I will accept him as a day boy."

That was it. Gabriel managed to purchase a small cottage with servant's quarters, close to the school. A pony and trap were also purchased but left with a caretaker until Ann returned.

"You'll need a driver and a maid, Ann, do you want any more servants?"

"No, Gabriel, that will be more than adequate."

Back at the plantation and it was all hustle and bustle as Matthew and his entourage were made ready for the trip back to Boston. A newly married young man that had shown promise driving the carriage was asked if he and his wife would like the job. Of course they did and were even more amazed when Gabriel drew up the papers giving them their freedom.

"Miss Hathaway has authority to sign those at the appropriate time. You must look after Matthew and her while they are in the school, and then you can return here as free men or remain in the North."

Buckets of tears eased when Gabriel promised they could return home for every school holiday.

The first night that Matthew was away, Joshua came to Gabriel.

"I know that to complete your happiness, Gabriel, you would like to make love to me completely. I will never be able to show you in any other way my deep love and respect for you and my gratitude for what you are doing for my family, so tonight I want you to bury your cock in my arse the way you have always wanted to."

Nearly 23 years old wasn't too old to cry. The tears of happiness would have almost floated a boat before Gabriel pulled himself together and ordered hot water for a bath. The two of them would fall into bed squeaky clean, and Gabriel would take them both off to Paradise.

Chapter 6

Josh and Gabriel had been lovers for three years with Joshua being the top. Gabriel had always led the lovemaking because he needed to show his love for this friend by lavishing affection on him. Josh always had the most amazing orgasms either from a blowjob or from planting his cock deep inside Gabriel's other end. He had never made love to a girl, he just thought that was the proper thing to do. One day he would find out and then he might have problems joining Gabriel in bed, but that was not a worry this particular night.

Stretched out on the bed he watched his friend. The eyes were filled with tears as he started to kiss and caress Josh, starting with the face. The words were what he expected, words of love and devotion. Josh stroked Gabriel's hair and face and replied in the same vein.

"I'm sorry I'm not like you Gabriel, but I do enjoy what you do to me, and even more, what you allow me to do to you. I hope I will tonight as well."

Gabriel continued to kiss Josh, slowly working his way down his body. He loved to play with Josh's nipples and spent a long time licking, kissing and nibbling them on this night. He took a fold of skin underneath his rib cage and gently nibbled that, working his way round the cage. He had never done that before and Josh loved it, making gentle cooing sounds to show his pleasure, down to the first prize, Josh's groin area. Gabriel could lay there and suck on Josh's balls and cock all night he loved it so much. That was when he got his first mouth full of cum.

At 23 years old, Josh had no problem returning to an erect state within minutes because of the continued stimulation from Gabriel's mouth. Then the action moved to a new level. Gabriel moved round to be between Josh's legs, spreading them wide and bending them. His tongue started just behind Josh's balls and worked its way back across the perineum to the anus, there it stopped and licked until it was quite wet before using his hands to spread Josh wider so that he could stab at the pretty entry to Paradise just being able to touch on the soft pink skin inside the entrance.

The tears now left Gabriel's eyes as he prepared to open him up, one finger fully embedded and working in and out made Josh's eyes open as wide as they ever had. The feelings as Gabriel managed to find and worry his g spot and Josh had never felt such extraordinary sensitivity. His cock was so hard it hurt.

By the time Gabriel had increased to four fingers Josh was panting. Gabriel lubricated them both and gently pushed his cock head into Josh's anus. The pain was quite intense despite Gabriel being so gentle, he felt Gabriel orgasm almost instantly amazing Josh, but with no change to his hardness. Gabriel fucked Josh slowly for ages, tears of pure joy coursing down his face. Josh watched his friend and knew that he had made the right decision.

'I will do this for him every day if he wishes,' was Josh's thought. He felt no animosity or disgust at the action that he was allowing, just a great love for this unusual white man who was more like a brother even than his real brothers.

Josh was quite sore before Gabriel was sated. He had orgasmed so many times that Josh was sure his balls must be empty. What amazed him was that he also had cum twice without touching himself. Gabriel licked up all the cum on Josh's chest before speaking.

"That is the nectar of the Gods, Josh, as sweet as anything I have ever tasted. I will love you forever for this gift."

Josh turned over, snuggled in close to Gabriel, not worrying about the sticky mess on Gabriel's cock, and before either young man knew it, the sun was shining through the windows and it was time to arise. Still spooned into Gabriel, Josh spoke when he knew Gabriel was awake.

"You are a wonderful lover, Gabriel, I hope it was good for you as well."

Gabriel laughed as he almost bounced out of bed.

"You have spoilt me for any other man, Josh, I will never make love to another being with the same joy you brought me last night."

Josh hopped out as well and planted a definite 'I love you' kiss on Gabriel's lips.

Washed and dressed they appeared in the dining room for breakfast and Sarah knew that something special had happened during the night, Gabriel had never looked so happy when he and Josh walked in. She knew, of course, of her son's peccadillo and accepted it without too much heart searching. Her love and pride in him was boundless.

The only cloud on the horizon of Gabriel's life now was the increasingly vitriolic speeches against the Union. He was sure that slavery would have to end one day. It wasn't practical for men and women to be owned by other men, regardless of their colour.

His reaction to all this was to buy even more gold with his plantation earnings. If it came to war he doubted paper money would be very useful to either side in comparison to precious metal. For ready use money he took payment in silver dollars.

Chapter 7

The election of Lincoln to the presidency put the final nail in the coffin of slavery as far as Gabriel was concerned. Not to be proved wrong, Confederate troops took Fort Sumter from the Union and the civil war became a reality. Gabriel then accepted no payment for his cotton in anything other than gold or silver, but that was for only one crop.

A naval blockade closed off his market and the crop of 1862 was left to rot in the warehouse, apart from the small amount that Sarah and her ladies turned into cloth for clothes and household furnishings. That gradually expanded into a full blown weaving plant that made cloth for sale as well as for the slaves. The Confederacy bought much of it and paid in confederate currency, useless for anything outside of the area, but it did at least purchase whatever they needed that was still available. A spin off from that was no hassle from confederate troops

"We can't sell it, Gabriel, so we'll use it," Sarah told Gabriel one day.

Food started to become a problem, or more precisely, lack of it became the problem. The war started to hurt in other ways. It became impossible for Matthew and the servants to return home during school holidays so Gabriel did the only thing he could. He found an underground group that would smuggle slaves out to the North. Once it was all planned he called a meeting of his four black foremen, Oprah and Landon, Sarah and Josh.

"We all know what is happening beyond our land and I think we need to take action to protect ourselves. I am going to free all slaves, I believe that will happen anyway when the war ends."

There were gasps of surprise from all.

"Josh, you will draw up the manumism papers for every slave on this plantation. Zeke, you will talk to all the slaves in the village. What you need to do is start fencing plots of land behind your cottages. Make them large enough to be able to grow food for the families. The bachelors and single women must do the same. When the plots are fenced I'll sell them to you all, along with your cottages, and the money to pay for them will come out of the wages I will pay. You will all have an account at the shop, purchases once again coming from your pay. Somehow or other we are going to get hold of enough seed for you to grow your vegetables and enough chickens and other animals for your other food. Anyone have anything to add or questions?"

Everyone was dumb struck.

"Mother, we'll take a bunch of the young bucks and single girls to do the same here at the big house. We must move to total self-sufficiency as soon as we can. Zeke, make it clear to all that if any of them want to leave they can do so, and when the war is over they will be welcome back here if they have found nothing better in the meantime."

This was all too much for the slave foremen and when they left the meeting their heads were aching trying to assimilate the tasks that had been set them. The group remaining was even more shocked with Gabriel's continued plans.

"Landon, you are going to take the remainder of your family through enemy lines to join Matthew and Ann in Boston. We will find a way for you to carry enough gold and silver to survive and for Ann and the others."

Joshua was the only one who didn't look shocked. He knew that in the secret room there was a huge quantity of gold and that in the study here there was probably enough silver to fund this action as well.

"I am going to send Blaine with you because he is big enough to fight off most likely trouble. Landon, you and Blaine are going to get in loads of practice with pistols and I'll arm you before you leave. Mama, I'd send you and Josh as well, but I doubt you would go, either of you."

They both shook their heads to confirm that.

"One side or the other will probably try to recruit the able bodied men into the army so we must make sure that if any soldiers come onto the plantation that all our men are either hidden or supplied with good enough stories and disguises to make sure they can remain free."

Joshua looked at Gabriel and grinned.

"You haven't just come up with this plan have you, Gabriel?"

Gabriel smiled. "No, Josh, I've been looking at what's happening and gradually put this plan together. I don't believe the South can win. It may take some time but I think the industrial strength, and size of the Union States will tell in the end. The South will be torn apart and I want to make sure our people stand every chance of surviving, and starting new lives as free men at the end of it. We'll close the house down as well so that it looks uncared for and partially unoccupied. Mother and I can manage with a tiny corner. Everything we can do to protect this for our future must be taken."

The plantation burst into life then as all the new activity took place. Gabriel's plan for Joshua's family was finalised. Heavy cloth was made into money belts for the grownups and the children. On the day they were due to start their journey the belts were filled with silver dollars and strapped round the bodies of the carriers. Guns and powder were in the hand baggage.

Everyone was briefed and Joshua and Jess accompanied them on the first stage of the journey. Jason and Missy were so excited, not realising how dangerous the journey was going to be.

Almost three months elapsed before Gabriel received positive news on the group. They had made the journey unharmed and unmolested. Ann had taken charge of all the money, paid for an extension to the cottage so that they could all live together. Landon and Oprah had got work and Ann was tutoring, keeping Jason and Missy educated as well. En route, before crossing into safe territory, Blaine had shot a confederate soldier who had tried to molest Oprah. He would never be able to return south and Gabriel placed that at the back of his mind to handle at the appropriate time. Blaine was the keeper of the family's security.

The young couple that had gone with Ann in the beginning were given permission to find their own future knowing that Gabriel's Hope would be open for them to return if they ever needed to. Gabriel realised that with so many men under arms, employment would be easy and he breathed a sigh of relief that the money he sent would probably be enough to last almost indefinitely, supplemented by the earnings of the others.

The first loss, and one that Gabriel had contemplated was the loss of their horses. The Confederacy would need an almost endless supply of them to replace the ones so cruelly lost in the battles and skirmishes that raged back and forth across the land.

The loss was conducted in a civilised manner. A young lieutenant with four troopers, already herding quite a few horses entered the plantation one day as Gabriel was riding back from looking at the work fragmented over the whole plantation.

"Good morning, Lieutenant, to what do I owe this visit?"

The officer, a little younger than Gabriel, looked embarrassed, not expecting to see a man of Gabriel's stature sat astride a fine stallion and dressed casually in high boots, breeches, and an open necked white shirt.

"I'm sorry, Sir, but I have come to purchase all of your horses for the army."

Gabriel looked at him carefully before replying.

"All of my horses, Lieutenant?"

"Yes, Sir."

"Where are you garrisoned?"

The lieutenant looked a little bemused but replied.

"About ten miles north of here, Sir."

"Well, Lieutenant. I'll strike a bargain with you. I have eight mounts that will probably suit your purpose. I'll sell you six. You take them back to your base and return here with one of them hitched to a wagon. I'll fill that wagon with fresh food and we'll consider that a deal."

"I could take all eight, Sir, and the food."

"That you could, but it would cost you more men than you will likely lose to the Yankies. I'll not see you or the Union troops destroy my home."

The lieutenant was taken aback.

"You would fire on your own people?"

"You're not my people, Lieutenant, you're one of the mongrels that is fighting a war you can't win for a cause that was lost before you even started it."

"But you have nearly a hundred slaves here I would guess."

"I don't have one slave on this plantation, every one of the men is free to take his family and go if he so wishes. They remain because they are paid and looked after."

Just as he finished that little speech, Zeke and two other men came into sight sporting a pair of pistols each, stuck into their waistbands.

"Zeke, tell this officer how many slaves there are on this plantation."

"Slaves, Mr. Gabriel, I haven't seen a slave on this plantation for longer than I can remember."

Poor Zeke, he had such a short memory.

"I'll have to ask my commanding officer, Sir, but I'll take the six and pay you for them."

The price was very low, and in Confederate currency, almost worthless in Gabriel's estimation.

"I only take payment in silver or gold, Lieutenant."

That was too much for the lieutenant. He rode out saying he would be back with his senior officer.

Gabriel's preparations for that were to dress several of his men that were adequate marksmen, to look like veterans of the fighting, but all looking as though they were unfit for further service.

A few hours later a major turned up with the lieutenant and ten troopers. He was met by Gabriel still riding his stallion, but now with two pistols in his belt, and six men, including Zeke equipped with the same.

"Mr. Sinclair, I am commanded to commandeer horse for the army. You have eight and I intend to take them."

"Major, I can probably manage with just two, leaving six for the army. I look after about one hundred souls on this plantation and produce food in sufficient quantity to feed them and leave some over for other deserving peoples. I won't see my people suffer to supply a lost cause."

The major bristled at this treasonous talk and told Gabriel so.

"Major, let's not fight over this. I am sorry to see my beloved land trodden down by the Yankee boot but the fact of the matter is that slavery was dead before a bullet was fired in this conflict. All that you are doing is prolonging the end with no chance of winning. The industrial North was always going to win, both in industrial output and in manpower. If I can preserve Gabriel's Hope from the ravages of this war at least a small corner of this land will be able to assist the rest to gather themselves again. My offer still exists, a wagon load of food and six of my horses."

The major looked at the armed Negroes and thought he had better use some serious good judgement on this.

"I have no silver or gold, Sir, but I will accept your offer and pay in confederate dollars with a small extra payment for the food."

Gabriel agreed, gave the nod to Zeke who had Isaiah bring six horses from the paddock. It was quite obvious that Gabriel's mount was the best of the bunch, a superb thorough bred stallion and the major looked at it with covetous eyes.

"Major, the cost is more than you and your troopers would be willing to pay, but I'll make you a promise. When the war has ended if you bring a mare to this plantation and we have survived, I'll let my stallion mount your mare and you can keep the result." The two men shook on a deal that made sense to the major.

The war raged around them and affected them very little until the day the first Union troops entered the property. Led only by a sergeant they were intent on robbing, pure and simple. Sarah was the first one they saw and started to molest her as Gabriel turned the corner of the house and spoke.

"That would be a very unwise move, Sergeant."

Half a dozen guns immediately turned on Gabriel who didn't even flinch.

"I am unarmed, Sergeant, so tell your men to point their arms elsewhere."

While he was talking, Gabriel had moved further along the porch until he could reach the warning bell he had installed for just this purpose.

Gabriel had just taken hold of the bell rope when the sergeant struck him across the face. It was perfect for Gabriel who could make the ringing of the bell look like an accident. By the time Gabriel had recovered there were a dozen black men each holding twin pistols pointed at the soldiers.

"Now, Sergeant, tell your men to put down their arms and we'll leave you all alive." The sergeant didn't need to say anything, his men dropped their arms.

"Zeke, bring some more boys and tie up these men."

The sergeant blustered but soon there were six troopers tied to the hitching rail in front of the house.

"When do you expect an officer to join you, Sergeant?"

"Sooner than you are going to want, because when he does there will be a whole troop behind him."

Gabriel nodded turned to Zeke and told him the men could return to work, and then he winked. The men disappeared behind the mansion but entered through the kitchen door and positioned themselves at windows and at the front door ready to enter the fray again if required.

Nearly an hour later, a large body of men moved through the main gate and formed up in front of the house. An officer looking less than pleased walked up to Gabriel with a drawn sword.

"I would put that away before getting any closer, Captain, a sword is no competition for two pistols," and Gabriel put his hands on his but didn't draw them. The Captain agreed and did put his sword back in his scabbard.

"Would you like to tell me what my men are doing tied to your hitching post?" and looking round continued, "And how did you achieve it?"

"Your sergeant started molesting my mother, not the action of an honourable man, so we had to show him the error of his ways. You can take him with you when you leave, Captain, and the rabble he came with. If they are a sample of Union troops I might start wishing for a Confederate victory."

"You mean you aren't now?"

"Let me show you why not, Captain."

The Captain was amazed as he walked through the village with Gabriel, who had carefully concealed his stallion beforehand.

"These people are all free, and you can see, happy. If the Confederacy wins, I will be under pressure to employ only slaves and these people will be forced to leave or become slaves again. I don't want that."

"Confederate troops won't like that, Sir."

Gabriel laughed, "They didn't, but if we go back to the house I'll show you what happened to them."

Stood in front of the house again Gabriel called, "Zeke, all ready."

The Captain stood mouth agape as the main door opened and he was confronted with twelve pistols and two more appeared at each of the downstairs windows.

The captain laughed as Gabriel brought his little army out in full view.

"A slave army to protect your land. I like it, Sir."

"No, Captain, these are all free men with families in the village you have just seen."

"Thank you, Zeke, the men can all return to their work."

Zeke looked with suspicion at the troops, and said, "Are you sure, Mr. Gabriel?"

"I think so, Zeke." And then he laughed.

"Now, Captain, what do you want me to do with your men, the ones that are free and my six prisoners?"

The captain could see the humour in the situation.

"I would like my free men to set up camp in one of your fields, Sir, and if you have any spare food we would surely like to purchase it."

"With what currency, Captain?"

"Silver dollars, Sir."

Gabriel grinned, put out his hand and introduced himself.

"Gabriel Sinclair, Captain, owner of Gabriel's Hope Plantation."

A firm hand grip and, "Captain Clinton Grant, Union Army."

Gabriel called out, "Joshua, Zeke."

The two men appeared from the house.

"Josh, Captain Grant will send his quartermaster to you. Will you sell him whatever they need? Zeke, you have inventory don't you?"

"Yes, Mr. Gabriel."

The captain was surprised at Joshua's appearance. He was dressed identically to Gabriel. Tailored riding breeches tucked into high polished riding boots and an open necked white shirt of fine quality cotton.

"Josh, the payment will be in silver dollars, so be kind to them."

"Not too kind though, Gabriel, hey."

Both men laughed and the Captain summoned his quartermaster while he tried to get his head round what looked like equals talking only one black and one white.

The captain took the opportunity to brief two subalterns concerning setting up camp.

"Abe, show the lieutenants the lower field, it's closest to the stream so they'll have plenty of water."

"Come, Captain, I'm sure my mother will be pleased to serve us some refreshment."

The Captain was impressed with the large kitchen where all the activity of the house appeared to take place.

"Most of the house is uninhabitable now, Captain, so we live in the kitchen."

All lies of course but Gabriel wasn't going to risk this army, or any other army, taking over the house.

After cool drinks and shortcake the captain was Clinton and Gabriel was also being called by his first name.

"Gabriel, my father is coming from the West with the largest army we can muster. This will be the end of the Confederacy when he arrives, Lee won't be able to hold him this time."

Gabriel nodded. "I pray that the battle doesn't rage over this land. I have kept most of my workers fed and housed during the war, and we are still well found for food. We will feed as many of your men as we can, but I will fight any army that tries to rob me of the food I need for my people."

Clinton smiled." I'll remember to tell my Colonel when he arrives with the remainder of our regiment. Now, Gabriel I should get back to my troops. May I take your prisoners with me?"

Both men laughed but through his laughter Gabriel managed to splutter, "Yes, Sir, you may."

"One last question, Gabriel, to satisfy my curiosity. "Joshua could have been a white man the way you two react to one another. How come?"

Gabriel decided he liked this man enough to be truthful.

"I have known Josh since I was aware of other people. His father is the only father I have ever known, and his mother is like a second mother to me. He has three siblings, and the whole family is safely in Boston. I educated Josh, teaching him each day what I was taught. He is now the estate managing accountant and my right hand man. On a personal front, he is the dearest person in my world."

Enough said and peace reigned on Gabriel's Hope.

The plantation didn't escape in the final days of the war, it raged over the plantation destroying much of the infrastructure including the great house which burnt to the ground. By some miracle the village survived, probably partly due to the inhabitants refusing to be driven out, the other miracle was Gabriel's beloved stallion, 'lost' in the trees of the plantation in the company of Fernando.

The war ended and the South sat back to breath and wonder at the destruction. The carpetbaggers moved in and a second war started for most plantation owners. They had to find a way to keep the carpetbaggers from stealing their land, and to rebuild with no assets to do it with.

Gabriel was lucky. Taking stock of the situation he realised how lucky they were. Yes, he would have to rebuild the house, but most of the valuables had joined the gold in the secret room, and as the war drew close almost everything that they could was moved into the room as well, the plantation had effectively survived.

The fields looked like a battle field, but he still had all, or nearly all of his workers. Replacing the men and women of the village would have been the most difficult task, these were people he knew, who knew him and would work hard to put their home and workplace back in order.

Two very pleasant things occurred while he was still in the planning stage of the rebuild. Clinton Grant, now a major, reappeared before returning to the North and his home.

"I have come to take my leave, Gabriel, and to offer my apologies that your home was destroyed. Also, my thanks for your hospitality. I have told my father of your kindness and assistance so if you ever need a favour, I am sure he would grant it."

The next day the Confederate Major appeared with a brood mare and stayed for two days while Gabriel's stallion did his job.

Chapter 8

"Mama, we'll live in Landon and Oprah's cottage for now and start rebuilding the big house. We have the sawmill and we can make our own bricks. We'll build on the original foundations and unless you want to change anything we'll rebuild it as it was."

"But where will the money come from?"

Joshua and Gabriel looked at each other and nearly fell over laughing.

"Oh, Mama, we are still wealthy. Almost all of our liquid assets were in gold and silver, we still have it all hidden. We'll fetch out as much as we need when we need it."

Sarah looked at the two men and shook her head.

"I might have guessed that my two clever sons would have planned for the worst when the war started."

Gabriel was still laughing as he told Sarah. "We had planned the disposal of my gold almost a year before war broke out, Mama, I was sure there would be war and that the South would lose."

Joshua couldn't speak he just looked at Sarah mouth agape. Sarah saw it and took him in a hug. "Didn't you know that is how I think of you?"

Joshua shook his head and cried.

"I am a silly thing, I thought that the love I have always shown you was enough. Of course I think of you as my son, but I share you the same as I share Gabriel with Landon and Oprah."

No more needed to be said, priority was on getting accommodation ready for as many as was needed. The overseers' cottages were the easiest to achieve before starting on the big house. Zeke and his men started preparing the fields for planting. Abe and his men worked on all the maintenance and repairs. The ladies continued to make cloth and clothe the plantation people first before offering it to traders in the town. Earning money was important now to throw people off the scent of where all the money was coming from to reconstruct.

The war had ended two months before when Gabriel spoke to Josh about a serious matter.

"Josh, how would you like to go to Boston to collect your family?"

"Seriously, Gabriel?"

"Mmm, Matthew and Ann can return if need be, but I would like to see them all back here for a while. In fact, all of them can return if that is their wish."

The usual game with money belt to protect his assets and Joshua was on his way. The tail he told when he came back was enough to bring tears to the eyes of Gabriel and Sarah.

"The destruction of the Southern states is monumental, Gabriel, it will take a generation to rebuild, always assuming there is the money to do it."

That sad news however was over ridden by the joy in seeing Matthew and the rest of the refugees. Gabriel couldn't resist, the young man might be too old for this but Gabriel didn't care, he lunged at Matt, picked him up and swung him round before holding him close and kissing him on the lips.

"I have missed you the most this last three years, Mattie."

Matthew looked flustered to start with, and then his memory kicked in and he remembered the good times with his white brother.

"And I've missed you, Gabriel, I love you."

Gabriel glowed and kissed him again. "I love you too, little man."

All of the others got hugs and kisses as well.

"I am so happy to see you all home. I bet it will take me weeks to hear all of your stories, but for now, let's get you settled. Landon, your family are where you were before. Mother and I have moved into the cottage next door. Ann, you have the cottage next door to that, your girl is waiting there for you. I think we should all eat tonight in your house, Oprah, if you will allow it."

"Oh yes, Gabriel, that will be fine."

The dinner really was a celebration and the only cloud that could have moved over it was accepted without any problem.

"Where are you going to sleep, Joshua? There is no room here now that the little ones are not so little."

"Mama, I am going to sleep where I have slept most nights in the past three years, with Gabriel. I don't think that will change any time soon either, even when the big house is rebuilt."

The two men looked at each other and the remainder of the people at the table knew, even if they hadn't done before. Joshua knew that night as well after that statement. He meant it, a woman was now most unlikely to move him from Gabriel's bed, and he accepted Gabriel's penis in his anus with joy.

The next day, as with every day since the end of the war, every able man and woman was working. The fields and gardens were the first priority, but then the building of the big house.

The stories from Boston had to wait until the evenings to be told. Matthew's was the first one.

"I was very frightened to start with, Gabriel. All of my classes were white and four years older than me. I think I was a novelty to start with, and by the time I might have expected to be bullied I had a champion. He remained my champion all through school even when I moved up faster than him. He was a big boy and made it clear that if anyone touched me he would beat them to a pulp. His name was Johnson and his grandfather is a senior politician. When I moved to college at eleven I was the wonder boy so nobody bothered me."

Matt laughed then and received another hug from Gabriel.

"Ann, tell us about your trip from here."

"It was quite frightening, Gabriel. When we were close to the front line of the troops we had to do much twisting and turning to avoid the patrols, particularly the Confederacy. We were eventually apprehended by a Union patrol and taken before a high ranking officer. I told him who we were and where we were going, and why. He was most surprised about Gabriel's Hope Plantation being worked by free blacks. When I told him that the owner looked on Landon as his father and Oprah as second mother he became most solicitous and arranged transport to take us the remainder of the way to Boston. We wrote to you immediately, but Sarah told Oprah that it took three months to reach you. Luke and Ruth stayed for a few months, but it was very crowded in the cottage so they eventually said they would like to seek a new life in the West. We've heard nothing since."

Gabriel tried to sound upbeat.

"They were young and eager, I'm sure they'll make it. They know they will always be welcome back here so they have that to fall back on if they need it.

The next evening would uncover more stories but during the day, Gabriel and Josh were on site as they cleared the foundations for the new big house. The stone chimney stacks had survived the fire and after careful application of acid to clean the stone and check them, it was decided to leave them in place. The gap between the two fireplaces in the study and dining room was passed off as an air space for help in preventing anything but the largest fire from engulfing the whole property. Gabriel and Joshua both knew that the trapdoor and staircase were ok and the gold room was secure because they had used it to withdraw some of the money required to order new equipment.

With everything under control on Gabriel's Hope, Gabriel started meeting other plantation owners that had survived the war, to talk. He was surprised that almost to a man they had been caught out and their wealth had all gone when the bank collapsed financially.

"I took my gold and buried it," Gabriel told them. "We have now used it to order new equipment and seeds for the cotton."

Obvious envy from the owners that were ruined got Gabriel thinking so he went to see Mr. Balfour.

"How easy would it be for me to start my own bank, Mr. Balfour?

"Seriously, Gabriel?"

"Yes, Sir. I was thinking of starting a trading company to supply other plantation owners with seed and equipment. They could pay for it with loans from my bank. I would set a fair rate of interest on the loans and make repayments conditional on the harvest. It is in all our interests to see the county prosper and as you know, I had a very good hoard of gold, which is intact."

"You would be seen as being very generous, Gabriel, at the same time, you can start making a second fortune as a merchant."

"I'm doing this for the family. I know that there will be resentment because I will make Joshua the manager of the bank. He is better with figures than I am and I think he would be more careful lending money than me because he would perceive that it was my money. He'll never accept my concept that it is family money, my mother and Joshua's family. I would need you to be very careful drawing up loan documents that would mortgage the plantations and properties of the borrowers."

Balfour laughed his dry lawyers laugh. "I guessed as much young Gabriel."

Leaving Balfour to sort out that problem, Gabriel needed to sort out Boston again. The cottage was still there with Blaine looking after it and the horse and carriage.

Summoning Matthew and Ann, Gabriel posed the question.

"What is your next move, and when?"

"If you have the money after this terrible war, Gabriel, Matthew has four more years at college. Then you and he will need to think about his future. He will only be fifteen but he will have a degree in finance and management. What he will lack is any kind of credibility, and that isn't just because of his colour."

"We have four years to worry about that, Ann, because the money is available for him to finish his education. Now, are you going back with him, and when do you have to go?"

"Yes, I want to go back with him and we have another two weeks."

"Good, two more weeks for me to spoil my little brother."

Nearly twelve years old with the maturity of a twenty year old, but he nearly crumbled at that comment.

"I can't decide who I love the most Gabriel, you, or Joshua? I know that it is your great love for Joshua that has made all of this possible so it is difficult for me."

Gabriel laughed and then got very serious.

"Let me tell you the whole truth, Mattie. My father deserted my mother and so did her family. Miss Sarah had to work very hard to feed me and keep a roof over our heads. Until I was five, I was virtually brought up by your mother and father while my mother worked. After that they still behaved like parents, loving me and helping me. They recognised my love for Joshua and never stopped us both being what we have become. I love Joshua as my brother and much more. I love you, and Jason and Missy like I love Joshua, well the brotherly part anyway."

Matthew interrupted that with a belly laugh, "I'm glad you said that last bit Gabe or I might have snuggled into bed with you tonight instead of Joshua."

Gabriel looked at Ann, who was looking in shock at Matthew, then at Gabriel, and then all three dissolved in silly giggles.

"I need to be careful what I say in front of this young man don't I, Ann. To finish, before I was so rudely interrupted, your parents are like my own, so what I am doing for you is as a brother, but I could change all that by turning you back into a slave to pay for it all."

More laughter and Gabriel had a lap full of boy, the same as he had done on occasions years before.

"I love you, Gabriel, I'll always love you and try to make you proud of me."

"I know you will, and I'll always love you as well. Now, Ann, have you met my new school teacher?"

Ann was surprised that Gabriel had bothered, with all the turmoil caused by the war.

"She is a black girl from the north who came south to try to find family. She took the job and looked for family in her spare time. They were killed in Atlanta, she found out, and now she is permanently here to teach all the children openly."

Ann was delighted and spent days with the new teacher, helping and advising. It was a happy/sad time until the parting when too many tears were shed.

"Remember, Mattie, you will be back at the end of every semester. Tell Blaine we won't forget him when the time comes for you all to return home. I'll try to find some way for him to come as well."

There was so much to do on the plantation that Gabriel had to cede all work on the new bank to Joshua and Mr. Balfour.

When the new bank building was complete, armed guards escorted the gold back to the town where it was deposited in a new safe. The bank opened its doors to start trading and immediately started to sign new customers that had some money. The rumours about Gabriel's wealth meant that everyone considered it a safe place for their money.

Joshua's presence as manager caused much resentment to start with that dissipated as quickly when people realised how competent he was and how friendly, always sloughing off any slight on his colour, never letting that influence his decisions on loans.

The county became an oasis in a sea of ruined estates and towns and within a year was one of the few areas that had started producing cotton again. Gabriel was sad that many of the plantations were treating their black workers no better than they had treated their slaves, and wondered if he could make it a condition of loans that the owners change that. Final decision, it was too radical to attempt. What he did do though was talk to these owners in a social environment about the improvement in productivity from happy workers. Gabriel's Hope was the plantation that showed the efficacy of that policy. The rapid building of the big house produced a short term problem.

"Mama, we will soon have an empty house. How are we going to fill it?"

Sarah laughed. "All in hand, Gabriel, I am shortly going to ask you to transfer quite a large sum of money to a New York bank and then Oprah and I are going to buy all the furniture and fittings for the house. If you will allow it we'll take Jess and Fernando with us."

"You won't need everything Mama, Josh and I will have a surprise for you if you leave us for a while."

Josh and Gabriel brought up all the house treasures from the secret room and displayed them round the study. Sarah was delighted but had no idea how they had achieved it.

"We are magicians, Mama, we conjured it out of thin air."

Sarah was so happy to see heirlooms from her childhood that she thought lost in the fire. Gabriel was so pleased, both men could be spared, and when Fernando got back he would think about finding some more horses. Perhaps it was time to think about breeding them instead of slaves. Good quality horseflesh, he felt, would soon be in demand from the small number of people starting to make money. He would be fuelling a whole economy the way things were going.

Chapter 9

The next four years appeared to fly. Gabriel's Hope was fully restored and producing its pre-war quantity of cotton. The paucity of producers kept the price high with the result that the gold and silver reserves in the bank kept increasing. Other plantation owners were slower to make money because their productivity was lower, confirming Gabriel's belief that happy workers were more productive. All this produced more money because loans were paid off more slowly.

Joshua had a new assistant, temporarily, his brother Matthew. Matt had knowledge of finance and management far greater than anyone else in Gabriel's sphere and that needed harnessing. He would have to get past the fact that the boy was only fifteen, black, and his adopted little brother. This was a man with huge untapped assets.

Sinclair trading, the bedrock of Gabriel's trading empire, was under the management of Jess, now with lots of input from Matthew.

A wagon company had been formed to transport all the goods being traded and because horses were a major part of that, Gabriel had educated Fernando, who, with the help of a clever young white man, was running the transport. Dick Turner was a young Englishman that had come out to America when the war ended thinking he could find work and start to make his fortune. Gabriel had come across him while out on business and offered him a job because at that time Fernando had not been educated to the level needed for the job. Now the two of them were running the company together.

Money talks and with some placed in the right hands, Blaine was given a new identity and was able to return to Gabriel's Hope. That caused a problem for Gabriel. He remembered the stupendous cock on his former butler and lusted after it again. Joshua wasn't stupid and realised that fact. When he needed to go to Washington to discuss moving some of the gold bullion there and bringing back silver dollars instead, he talked about it to Gabriel.

"I know how much you lusted after Blaine's cock when he was here before. I'm going to be away for a few days. Why don't you get reacquainted with it, I promise I won't mind. I think our love goes way beyond sex."

Gabriel made love to Joshua that last night with a passion that mirrored their early love making.

With Joshua gone, Gabriel had two reasons to think about Blaine. When was he going to have sex with him and what was he going to do with him now. Keeping him in the house was too risky, even with his new identity. Returning him to the fields would be unfair. In the end Gabriel decided the transport company would be best. He sent for him after supper that night and in the study asked him if he would be happy as a driver on the wagons. Blaine was delighted, he never expected any special treatment when he returned. It was easy then for Gabriel to suggest that they bath together and Gabriel then continued to the main event.

"I have never forgotten this appendage Blaine," he said when they were both naked and he could grasp it, "And tonight I want to play with it for a long time before you use it on me like you used to. That's always providing you don't mind."

Blaine smiled, "I don't mind, Mr. Gabriel, you know I'll do anything for you."

No more needed to be said, after the bath, Blaine stretched out on the bed and allowed Gabriel to play. Gabriel spent ages playing, sucking on the balls and stroking the cock, it was amazingly erotic for him. In the 69 position it left Blaine clear to slowly open up one very eager anus. The stimulation of Blaine finger fucking him while he sucked and played with the huge cock soon had Gabriel panting.

"Take me now, Blaine, I can't wait any longer."

Gabriel rolled over and came up on his knees with his legs well spread and his head and shoulders on the bed. Blaine lubed them both before placing his glans at the entrance to Gabriel's arse.

"Go ahead Blaine."

Gabriel bit down hard on the pillow he was resting on to stifle the scream as the pain hit him. It was some time before he could relax enough to tell Blaine to continue. Then it was incredible, the feeling as that huge cock moved in and out of him, penetrating a little more each time was stupendous. He took it doggy fashion for a little while before turning over and letting Blaine fuck him hard to orgasm. His own orgasms were mind bending in their intensity. That huge cock could so easily destroy his sanity.

When they were both cleaned up and calmed down, Gabriel surprised Blaine with his next piece of conversation.

"That was as good as I could wish for Blaine, I would like to do that again before Joshua returns and I would like your new boss to join us. You see, Fernando is like me and I know he would almost expire for the opportunity to feel you doing to him what you have just done to me."

Blaine was surprised, and then pleased, pleasuring his boss and his boss' boss could only be good for his future. He wouldn't take cock in his arse now that he was a free man, but he had no problem giving it. He might even consider giving a blowjob to either or both of them if they asked, but he wouldn't volunteer.

The next day, Gabriel had one of his usual talks with the people that ran his businesses. Mattie was on top of the business at the bank with Jess fronting everything. At the transport depot he sat with Fernando and casually mentioned the new driver.

"Fernando, the new guy is called Blaine, he used to be my butler at the house before the war and he looked after my family in Boston until they came home. He is now going to work for you. Look after him because I owe him a lot for protecting my family. Get to know him today and if you get on okay both of you bathe and come up to the big house after supper tonight. I want you to see what he carries between his legs and then if you like what you see I think we might be able to have some fun as a threesome because it is a long time since I felt your man rammer inside me and I'm sure you'll want Blaine to tickle your insides with his."

Gabriel was grinning and Fernando soon joined him. He didn't think very much about Blaine but he did remember the fantastic sex he had enjoyed with Gabriel for years. He still loved to fuck and be fucked as often as he could find a partner.

After supper, Gabriel had a word with Lucas, who was the new butler.

"Two of my transport people will be calling soon, show them up to my suite as soon as they arrive."

Lucas knew that Joshua slept with the master when he was here so he could only imagine what these two were going to be doing in the master suite instead of meeting in the study which would have been normal. Gabriel saw the quizzical expression and laughed.

"I don't think you would want to join us, Lucas, but know that you can if you want to."

Lucas looked quite shocked, "I don't think so, Mr. Gabriel, I'm sure Molly would be very upset if she found out."

Gabriel was going to get plenty of fun out of this if he could.

"You're probably right, but if you want to try it anytime, you can tell her I kept you late. I'm sure it would be okay when Joshua gets back as well because I know he thinks you are a very handsome young man."

Lucas scurried off then with lots to think about. He had heard about man on man sex and now he was being offered the chance to indulge, he wondered if it would be good. Perhaps he would talk to Joshua about it when he came back from Washington. He liked living in the bachelor house with the other men, but he also enjoyed Molly's company. He didn't have the urge to bed her, so, perhaps he should try man on man sex before making a final decision on relationships.

Gabriel thought about Lucas as he disrobed. He had employed him just after the new big house was complete and furnished. He was still very young but Gabriel thought it would be good to train him from scratch. He was a quadroon, almost white, so quite a feather in the cap for Gabriel when they entertained. He looked very handsome in the simple uniform that Gabriel still insisted on, fitted black trousers, with a fitted white shirt. It looked fresh and Lucas loved it.

The boy had no family, and when Gabriel found him begging in the street in Charleston when he was there on business one day seemed like too good a chance to miss. His transition from beggar to butler had been a joy to watch, the boy had a most engaging and deferential personality, exactly suited to his job. Molly fell in love with him despite her being a few years older than him. Now that there was no slavery Gabriel couldn't make the men shuck down, but he got round that problem by saying that he needed the boy naked to measure him for his new clothes. Gabriel made fun of it by doing it in the grounds close to the water.

Lucas wasn't at all embarrassed with the way Gabriel went about it so no resentment at this early nudity for his new job. In fact, he found it quite erotic undressing in the open air and sprung an erection, which did embarrass him until Gabriel made light of it and congratulated him on his lovely body and very attractive cock.

Gabriel stripped and slid into a dressing gown while he thought about this new possibility. Nearly at the end of his 20's he had not mellowed, he still loved cock, either end. Joshua knew, understood, and didn't worry. He knew he had all of Gabriel's love if not his lust, but their lovemaking was still a wonderful experience.

The knock on the door stopped the thoughts and he called, "Come in."

Lucas came in first, "Your guests are here, Mr. Gabriel."

"Thank you, Lucas. I won't need you anymore tonight."

Fernando and Blaine came in, both smiling.

"I presume you two have become friends today."

Fernando was grinning.

"Yes, Sir, I have made it very clear to our new driver that any mistakes and I'll take it out on his arse, and I don't mean with a whip. Depending on how satisfactory he is tonight I will probably offer mine as a reward when he does a good job."

Broad smiles all round was a good start.

"In that case, Fernando, why don't you undress our man and see what you think. In fact let's all get naked then we won't have any interruptions."

Watching Fernando's eyes was enough to make Gabriel have to smother his amusement.

"I think you should sit in the boss' armchair, Blaine, while I check out that equipment."

The following action had Gabriel monumentally hard. It was so erotic watching Fernando devouring Blaine's huge cock. He played with the balls, but his mouth hardly left the cock. He sucked on the glans, licked and masturbated the shaft but kept his mouth or tongue in contact with the cock all the time.

"Tell me when you are getting close Blaine. I want your first load in my arse, then we can both play with you to get you ready for Fernando. Fernando, you can open me up when Blaine is ready."

Blaine didn't take long with the mastery that Fernando showed, he had, after all, practised frequently with Gabriel.

This was so good, Gabriel was almost cooing. He played with Blaine while Fernando opened him up, it was marvellous but the best part was Fernando feeding him Blaine's cock, guiding it in, not that he really needed to. A few minutes of doggy fashion and then he was made comfortable on his back while Blaine fucked him with long slow strokes and he played with and sucked Fernando who was holding his legs back and wide. This was slutty sex like Gabriel could put up with every day. Blaine lasted well considering the eroticism of Fernando playing with him before. When he did orgasm, it was, as always, ferocious. He had to admit that fucking Gabriel was incredibly exciting for his cock. A quick clean up and then Fernando and Gabriel both went to work on Blaine.

There was so much cock they had no problem both playing. Gabriel left Fernando to it after a while and started to open up his transport manager ready for Blaine to go a second time. Gabriel was mesmerized watching the action. Fernando showed what a total cock slut he was. He was wriggling and moaning as Blaine slid in all the way on each stroke. Monumentally hard again, Gabriel couldn't resist and gave Fernando a blowjob that with the stimulation from his arse fucking brought him to a spine shattering orgasm that defied Gabriel's ability to swallow. He didn't waste it though, any that escaped he hoovered up with his mouth. The final act was for both black men to attack their boss and spit roast him with Fernando taking the arse.

Completely washed out afterwards, Gabriel did manage to say, "If my transport company is run with as much enthusiasm and enterprise as you show in sexual matters it will be more profitable than the plantation and the bank combined."

Much laughter after that comment and Blaine lay back and thought how much he owed Gabriel for sticking by him after the shooting and bringing him back to work here at he knew not what cost. Fernando was having similar thoughts. He would almost certainly have fallen foul of someone over his sexuality, but here he was managing a transport company as a free man and having great sex with his boss, and now this new man who had the most amazing cock. Could life really get any better?

"We might manage one more session like this before Joshua gets back from Washington and then I think I shall have to be a good boy again."

Blaine got all serious then.

"I don't think I could ever take a cock up my arse, Mr. Gabriel, but almost anything else you wanted from me you could have any time."

Fernando nodded his agreement and voiced it, "The same goes for me, Boss, but you can include the butt fucking as well, even if it is only a quickie."

Gabriel lay back and thought about it.

"Why don't we repeat this again then tomorrow night? Instead of me being the master why don't you take over Fernando? You can make it a little kinkier if you like, I'm not averse to a little slave punishment. I'm sure you know how to handle that from your time before you came to this plantation."

Both blacks looked at each other, remembering the beatings for minor mistakes or even no mistakes, just at the whim of the master or overseer, but never on this plantation.

"Out of curiosity, Boss, have you ever beaten a slave or saw one being beaten?"

"No to both, Fernando. I have seen slaves abused in town by uncaring owners but never a proper beating and I was never party to anything on this plantation until I became owner. I saw some of the scarred backs of slaves when I first came here but I sacked the white manager and overseers and put Zeke in charge. I don't think he ever beat a fellow slave and now of course they are all free men."

"And the best looked after free blacks in the county."

Gabriel blushed a little and then sent them on their way.

Time for bed and Gabriel was about to shed his robe to do just that when there was a knock on his door. Lucas was there looking a little unsure.

"Come in, Boy, what is it?"

"I have thought about what you said and I must admit, the two men that have just left are very attractive, and I thought I might like to try man on man sex, but just with you to start with, Mr. Gabriel, if you don't think I am being too forward."

Gabriel smiled and told the boy to sit.

"Do you know why I picked you out of the gutter and brought you to the plantation, Lucas?"

Lucas shook his head.

"Well, it was partly because I could see that you were very pleasing on the eye and that was something I wanted from my new butler. The second part was that despite having a wonderful companion in Joshua, I do like to have sex with other men and you are very attractive, so I hoped that you would like a sexual romp sometime, even if, like Blaine, you weren't a man lover."

Lucas was surprised that the master could have sex with a man that only did it for the master.

"In that case, will you have sex with me now, Sir, so that I can decide if I like it? I will do anything for you but I don't want to do it with anyone else until I'm sure."

Gabriel was delighted. This boy was ten years younger than him, but he was delightful to look at. He stood up, walked across to Lucas and pulled him out of his chair before planting a soft kiss on his lips.

"I promise I'll be very gentle with you, but I will make love to you going all the way. That is, I will finish by putting my cock inside your bottom."

Gabriel's cock was already starting to tent his robe so he just slid out of it.

"We are equal now, you have seen me naked and erect as I did with you in the grounds. Now I'm going to undress you."

Lucas was nervous but this man had rescued him from a miserable lifestyle and trained him for a position of importance in this grand house. He had good clothes on his back and money in his pocket, a full stomach and a warm bed to sleep in at nights. Most of his race were worse off than they had been as slaves.

The nervousness soon disappeared as Gabriel caressed his body, kissing his way down it, exciting the nipples first and then the unbelievable sensation of having his cock and balls sucked. He thought he was going to die the sensations were so overwhelming.

Things just kept getting better as Gabriel started to attack the anus, kissing and licking it before sliding the first finger in. Lucas slid further into a stupefied state ruled by the sensitivity and eroticism of Gabriel's actions. He came back to earth briefly as Gabriel slid his glans over his sphincter where he stopped for a minute or two as Lucas wriggled about, adjusting to the penetration. Gabriel continued and smiled with pleasure as he saw Lucas completely relax, get fully hard again, sigh with pleasure at the feelings racing round his body as Gabriel slowly fucked him to an amazing orgasm. Both men sated and Gabriel slid out of Lucas, rolled sideways, and took the boy in his arms. A few minutes to calm down and Lucas looked in awe as he spoke.

"That was amazing, Mr. Gabriel, I have never felt anything so exciting come even close to that in my life."

Gabriel kissed the boy again realising that the experience had pleased him immensely as well.

"I thought it was as well, Lucas, I think Mr. Joshua will have to join us for a threesome when he gets back, I'm sure he will find you as exciting as I did."

Lucas was so pleased, he had no idea man on man sex would be so incredible, and now he was likely to find out if Joshua was as good. He was sure in his mind that he would be because Joshua was incredibly sexy to look at. His mind racing, Lucas thought of Joshua's two brothers who were also very good looking. How likely was it that they would love boy/ boy sex as well? Not very. Ah well, the two he might have were marvellous to think about.

"Go and wash your private parts Lucas and then come and sleep with me."

The next morning Lucas realised that was the icing on the cake, sleeping snuggled up to Gabriel had been exquisite pleasure.

Joshua returned from Washington, well pleased with the deal he had made to relinquish some of the bank's gold in exchange for more easily manageable silver dollars.

Matthew had managed very well and despite his colour and age was being accepted by the bank's customers as something of a financial whizz kid. He was puting forward advice on money management that was saving the plantation and business owners much money.

Fernando and his white deputy were running transport with no problems. Occasionally, Gabriel would have to sign a requisition and payment for new wagons and horses and that was about all.

Jason, at 17, was very quickly coming up to speed taking over Joshua's job as accountant for the plantation. Missy was understudying the senior seamstress and starting to design her own clothes. The next step for her would be her own dress shop in town.

Chapter 10

Gabriel and Joshua hardly had time to celebrate their thirtieth birthdays, but they weren't worried. The constant in their lives made celebrations unnecessary. That was their continued great love for one another. Very few people that knew them were in any doubt that these two men loved each other like brothers, not knowing the reality. But when these two men had dragged the county out of war torn desolation into a vibrant and booming economy, it was almost unheard of anywhere else in the South, they weren't about to think about it overly much.

On the day that Grant became president, Gabriel, now with so much more time on his hands, started considering the idea of running for political office to try on a bigger stage to effect changes that would help reconstruction of the South. Now was the time to call in a favour, so he made contact with Clinton Grant.

The telegraphed message was received in Washington and Clinton wired back.

'Come to Washington, Gabriel, meet my father. I'm sure he will be very interested in securing you a seat in the congress. I will leave a message with the station master to direct you when you arrive.'

Gabriel showed this to Joshua and asked what he thought.

"If I go to congress, Josh, I'll be spending a lot of time in Washington."

"Go for it, Gabriel. Matthew and Jess will be able to run the bank in a year or two and I will be able to spend more time with you in the Capital."

Bags packed and Gabriel was on his way to a new adventure. The station master in Washington gave Gabriel his instructions. He was most surprised that it was to go to the White House. The cab was waved through the gate when Gabriel offered his name. A liveried servant showed him through to a pleasant salon where he was joined a few minutes later by Clinton Grant.

"Gabriel, welcome to Washington. It is so good to see you."

Gabriel was quite taken back by the enthusiastic welcome but replied in kind.

"Thank you, Clinton, it's good to see you as well. I can't thank you enough for fast tracking me to the White House."

Both men laughed.

"Come, I have rooms for you next to mine, the servants have taken your bags up already. We'll join father for dinner, tonight you are lucky, he actually doesn't have any engagements."

Thus began Gabriel's new adventure. The President was most impressed with Gabriel when he had finished quizzing him about his life and his post war achievements.

"I have heard much about you, Mr. Sinclair, initially from my son who you impressed when you held a gun to his head to protect your plantation and all of your workers."

Gabriel blushed and Clinton laughed.

"He was a demon, Dad. I think you can be glad he wasn't in the army, you might have had one hell of a fight on your hands to take South Carolina."

"My thoughts, Son. Mr. Sinclair, I think it would be a very good idea for me to ask the senator for South Carolina to stand down at the next election and allow you to take his place. I am sure you would romp home just on your record with York County. We are all talking about your success and wishing more of the South had applied themselves as your fellow plantation owners and business men have."

Gabriel was pleased but wanted to keep the record straight.

"Thank you, Mr. President, but I have achieved so much because I hid all of my gold assets away from your troops and was able to use it to the benefit of all that wanted it and were prepared to work for it."

The President laughed, "Yes, I've heard. There were many in congress that wanted your wealth confiscated for war reparation. I think even our Northern Court Judges might have baulked at allowing that when we knew your circumstances and your views on slavery and the war."

Gabriel remained as a guest of the president for several days, meeting influential politicians from both sides of the house. When he returned to Gabriel's Hope, he had a very good idea of what his life would be like as a senator. Mixed feelings were a good way to sum up his feelings. The relatively easy life of the southern business man would go and be replaced with the hustle and bustle of the Capital and the cut and thrust of politics. In his heart he knew he had to do it for the sake of his beloved South.

With one year to go before the next Senate elections, Gabriel set up a campaign headquarters in Charleston, booked a permanent suite of rooms in the best hotel and with much help from party headquarters set about recruiting staff and most important, fund raisers.

Time spent at Gabriel's hope now was for relaxation. As yet, no blacks had a vote so Gabriel knew he would have to pitch his campaign towards helping the regeneration of the South by harassing congress to make more funds available. His own wealth would be brought up he was quite sure, but he had facts and figures on hand to show how he had used that wealth to help many other businesses and plantations in York County by funding the bank and that he wanted to go to congress to try to broaden that aid.

"We aren't asking for charity, just the means to rebuild the whole of the South like we have with York County," was how intended to pitch his campaign.

His use of blacks in high profile positions would be his biggest drawback but he would have to show how they had more than justified his faith in them. He wasn't wrong in that assumption so he developed a story, telling his audience about his early life and how the only friends he had coming from the poorest part of town were the free blacks.

"I was never shown anything but support and friendship from these people who didn't take the colour of my skin into account when they helped me. Their reward when I became a wealthy plantation owner was to help them in the same way by ignoring their skin colour and focusing on their abilities and they have justified that trust. The blacks outnumber us whites, we will need those numbers if we are to rebuild our beloved South. We can't do it by ourselves. If you look after your black workers they will respond, as they have in York County. Now I want you all to share in that future, I'll even instruct my bank manager to lend to plantations and businesses outside York County but I don't have enough money to do it all. That's why I want you to send me to the Congress so that I can fight for you there."

"And line your own pockets as well no doubt."

That comment at one meeting really hurt Gabriel, he had never given a thought to his own status and possibilities for garnering more wealth and power. He just wanted to see his South regenerated. He had to make his reply robust so he looked at his accuser, not really seeing him while he focussed his mind.

"You're right. I will have the knowledge to further increase my wealth and influence. Now look at York County and tell me that is what I have done. Look at my bank's loan book and see how many plantations or businesses we have foreclosed so that I could take them over. See how many loans we have made on top of the initial funding to help struggling businesses rather than take them over. If I wanted more power and more wealth I wouldn't need to go to Congress, I can multiply my wealth much more easily right on my own doorstep. What I want to do, I want to do for you. Reject me and York County will still be an oasis in this desert instead of the oasis spreading."

That was the tone at many meetings and Gabriel sailed into Congress on a massive tidal wave of support.

Washington was frightening for Gabriel and without Clinton's help and support he may well have run back to Gabriel's Hope. The Congress was a home for bickering and endless debate with very few constructive laws being enacted. Furious at the lack of progress in rebuilding all of the States, not just the South, so infuriated Gabriel that he asked Clinton to get him in to see his father.

"Mr. President, I have sat for one year listening to endless, pointless debate about almost everything that the congress should have passed into law even before I came to Washington. They appear to have forgotten they are here to represent the people and to implement laws that will help those people. I feel I have achieved nothing and would only consider reversing my decision to resign if I could give the rest of the congress a collective kick in the butt.

I'm sorry, Sir, but I am going home to help my fellows because it is quite obvious Congress isn't going to."

Both Grants were disappointed with this news and tried for hours to make Gabriel change his mind to no avail. Clinton was the most upset, he had found a new and interesting friend in Gabriel Sinclair.

"You will both be more than welcome in my home if you ever make it to South Carolina but I doubt you will see me in this city again."

The next day, Gabriel headed for home, Gabriel's Hope and his beloved Joshua.

"I should never have gone, Josh, I have wasted a year of my life. Now that I know the Congress is no friend of the South I am going to devote even more time and money to rebuilding what the war destroyed.

I will start work tomorrow in the bank. I want to go through our loan book carefully, check the state of our deposits and the value of my personal holdings. Then I'm going to do the same with the plantation, the transport company and the trading company. Have Mattie there as well because if we can afford it I'm going to start expanding our loan book to other counties."

Joshua knew that Gabriel had the bit between his teeth and there would be no stopping him now. Their lovemaking that night was as satisfying as ever. Gabriel showed his soul mate how much he had missed him and left the pair of them soaked in sweat and adding to that wetness with tears of happiness at their reunion.

One week later, Gabriel sat down with Josh and Mattie in the study of Gabriel's Hope to discuss their findings.

"Stripping out other depositor's money and if I had to write off all of the loans we would still have more than $500,000 to play with and the companies are contributing all the time. I want to keep 20 percent of that for re-investment if we need to but the remainder I want to use as loan money for an expanding area. I thought I would start speaking to the electorate that sent me to congress and tell them my bank will look at loans to any that need it and can generate income from the loans to pay them back. Mattie, you and I have to investigate each applicant by doing on site checks. We'll make it a condition that they buy through my trading company and use my transport company to deliver whatever they need. We double check then make sure the money is going where they said it was and I'll look at young Dick going round occasionally to check that things are going as expected. He can be spared from the transport side for short periods, Fernando is very capable. Bad loans should then become a rarity and we'll have collateral anyway, not that I want to run anymore plantations or businesses."

The reality was that outside of York county many loans did go bad and Gabriel ended up owning several more plantations and businesses that he hadn't planned on. The result of this was that his management team was sorely stretched and the end result was his senior foremen from Gabriel's Hope being put in charge of other plantations and Dick was put in charge of two of the failed businesses to turn them around with excellent results forthcoming, running them on Mattie's plans. Zeke's co-foremen ran the new plantations the way Gabriel ran Gabriel's Hope with similar results.

Another five years passed with Gabriel building an even bigger business empire. Disadvantaged whites didn't like what they saw, successful blacks stuck in the craw of too many to ignore the possible repercussions. Intimidation resulted and Gabriel had no choice then. To protect his black managers outside of York County, he placed white men in the position of boss in each of the plantations. To keep his black overseers in charge in reality he brought young men in from England and the Northern States, gave them training at Gabriel's Hope before placing them in the other plantations giving them this instruction.

"My estate managers are all black, as are the overseers. That isn't going to change. You will continue to learn how to manage the plantation you are sent to, but you will make all decisions in consultation with the manager. Every week you will present a report of the week's work to myself or Dick Turner. All requisitions will be signed by you and the estate manager. The paperwork will be collected and on weeks when it is me collecting it I will take a tour of the plantation. To the outside world however you will behave as though you are in charge completely. Learn well because the next plantations that I take over will be run by yourselves as proper managers, so two of you to each plantation."

These young men had been recruited from organisations both in the States and in England that promoted equality for the Negroes.

By the time Gabriel and Joshua were forty, Mattie had virtually taken over the running of Gabriel's empire from his headquarters in York County. Dick Turner was General Manager of the group, Jess was manager of the bank and Fernando ran the transport company. Jason was now effectively estate manager of Gabriel's Hope and Missy had her own fashion complex in Charleston.

Gabriel felt he had worked hard enough and long enough with Josh and he was going to ease back and enjoy life more.

"Josh, I have one more project to develop and then I think we might do some traveling. On the strip of land to the South of the river, close to the water hole, I want to build an estate of houses. They are going to be the retirement presents for my four original overseers, Jess, Mattie, Missy, Fernando, and Jason if he wants one. If Dick Turner will live among Negroes I will build one for him as well or he can purchase in the market."

Oprah and Landon had retired but continued to live in the house Gabriel had given them the day he became master of the plantation. Sarah had trained Molly to be senior housekeeper and remained at Gabriel's hope until she died.

Josh, as always, accepted Gabriel's word without comment. He had grown used to Gabriel's generosity and just continued to grow his love for this exceptional friend.

The children on all plantations continued to be educated in keeping with the original idea with Joshua's siblings.

The Grants were regular visitors to the plantation, particularly Clinton who at last admitted to Gabriel that he was gay as well and had loved him since they first met. That love never took the shape of a sexual relationship because Gabriel and Joshua had become monogamous. He remained a loving friend until his early demise in a hunting accident.

Gabriel created a Trust for all of his assets and made Mattie the Chairman of the trust with Dick as his deputy. The provisions for distribution of funds from the trust were kept secret for fifty years after Gabriel's death because the foundation was set up to be run by, and look after the needs and wellbeing of the descendants of Joshua's siblings.

Mattie's Grandson was the first Negro to sit openly as chairman of the Sinclair Foundation, overseen by Mattie until his death in 1940 at the age of eighty.

THE END

Here is a sample from another story you may enjoy:

Chris Johns

A TRADE
for a Trade

Gay Romance Erotica

The only word I could think of as I looked at the training room and the trading floor next to it was, 'intimidating.' Today was the day I was going to start changing my life, and this is where I was going to start.

It all started about a week ago. On the underground going to work in my dead end job, I picked up a financial paper left by a previous traveller and started reading it. 'Become a Forex Trader,' an advert at the back said. It gave a website to go to for more information, so I tore the ad out and put it in my pocket. That night, I read all the blurb on the web, it sounded fantastic. I booked there and then for a seminar to lay out how I was going to develop the skills to earn a six-figure income in less than three years. The day of the seminar, I called in sick and went. Wow, what they showed us was amazing. The only problem was, it would take all my savings to buy the training.

At 20 years old, with a couple of decent A levels and not much else, I was never going to get a well-paid job unless I took a chance on something that could jump me out of my miserable existence. I handed over my credit card and saw my miserably small life savings disappear.

So, here I was in this amazing place, with little more than a determination to get through the next few days. While I waited for everyone else to arrive, I took in my surroundings and the people that populated it. The reception area was very plush with high tables and stools, a kitchenette with endless supplies of coffee, chocolate and tea. The trading floor was a mass of computer screens with loads of men and women working them, but all seemingly very laid back. I was looking at it through a glass wall. Next to it was the training room, also with a glass wall, it looked high-tech, which I found out very quickly was the case.

A few of the people who worked there looked to be in their 50s, a larger number in their 30s and three who only looked a few years older than me. All three of them were dressed to kill. I scoped them out thoroughly, hoping they had not seen where my eyes went. They looked good enough to eat and my cock stirred at the thought of getting at their bodies.

I had time for a coffee before we were ushered into the training room. The guy who stood to the lectern at the side of the giant screen was the dishiest of the three young guys. He was what I would call chunky. Not slim, but definitely not fat either. He was wearing a button down dress shirt, open at the collar. His designer jeans looked expensive and looked as though these, along with the shirt, had been moulded for his body. Great pecs and a juicy looking bulge at the crotch had me fully erect. I just had to hope I wouldn't be asked to stand up because there was no way my more than adequate man meat was not going to be noticed.

His name was Andy and during the course of the morning session, we found out he had come here straight from university three years ago, so, 24, I guessed. He now traded a personal six-figure account and a seven-figure one for a client. He traded once per day and when he wasn't lecturing, he lived in Ko Samui in Thailand with his Californian partner. It was some time before I found out that partner was same sex.

After the first session, the lecturer was the second one of the young guys. He was black, over six feet tall and well-built. I guessed his suit would have cost upwards to £750. Shirt and tie were great, completed with a pair of obviously hand-tooled leather shoes. He looked like a model for Saville Row Tailor. He delivered a psychology lecture as smooth as his looks and dress. He was almost as stunning as Andy and introduced himself as Lee, a couple of years older than Andy and already a senior trader. Like many of his race, he looked younger than his 26. Trousers tailored so that nothing of his manhood showed, but he was sexy.

Lunch was a buffet and meant to impress, it was superb. After lunch we had the third of the young guns. His name was Durgas, 29, and a Sikh. He was imposing. He wore a black turban, skin tight black T shirt, skin tight black designer jeans and patent leather shoes. Not much left to the imagination front or back.

All three of these guys had gorgeous arses, and Andy and Durgas had interesting bulges. I assumed that Lee would be the biggest because of his race. All three were fantastically good looking and spoke beautifully. I hoped in three years' time, I would look as good; the basics were there, I just needed the money to make it look as good.

I'm sure I made a fool of myself because for two days, I asked a gazillion questions and no one else seemed to ask any at all. End of the course and Lee approached me.

"Alan, I've been seriously impressed with your enthusiasm, so, I'm taking you as my student for your trading floor course. We'll be one to one for all the future sessions spread over the next few weeks. You have your trading account set up and funded, you have your trading platform, so go away and start trading. Remember your risk management, call the graduate line any time you have a query and I'll see you back here on Monday at 0900. We'll analyse your trades and spend the day together on the floor looking at more advanced methods of keeping the good ones going and leaving the bad ones behind."

I wondered what was going on. We were only allocated three sessions, not all day. Was I receiving special treatment for some reason?

If you enjoyed this sample then look for **A Trade for a Trade**.

Also by this Author

Brotherly Love

Underworld

Revenge of the Jocks

Indian Abduction

Pleasurable Abduction

Lost

A Grip in Deep

Bullet Holes

Gay Porn Star

Delightfully Yours

Embracing the Greener Side

Promotional Desire

Aviator's Hidden Turbulence

Almost Paradise

The Hardcore Remedy

Relish Pretender

Doctor Boner

Captivated Attractions

Academically Horny

Flight of the Hornies

About the Author

The author has drawn from his lifetime experiences as a Marine Engineer and Helicopter Pilot to take his readers round the world with his erotic stories.

Born in a small town in middle England he joined the Royal Navy straight from school and spent four years at engineering college before going to sea. After promotion to first engineer he took a career turn and trained as a helicopter pilot. The move afforded him huge opportunity to travel both as a Naval Pilot and later as a Commercial Helicopter Pilot. His Bio Pic was taken when he was relaxing in his company's social club, serving his fellow pilots and engineers with some excellent English Ale.

Retired now in the Caribbean he took up writing to compliment his other great love, sailing.

From the Author

If you want any more info about me, please feel free to ask! I'm a very open person so you won't offend me if you want to get more personal.

If you'd like to give me comments or suggestions to any of my books, feel free to shoot me an email at chris_johns@awesomeauthors.org.

Check my page on Amazon and my blog for Updates and interesting info.

Author Central – http://amzn.to/185Sar5
Author Blog - http://chris-johns.awesomeauthors.org/

If you enjoyed any of my books then please share the love and click like on my books in Amazon.

If you write me a review and send me an email I will send you a free book, or many.
(Just know that these emails are filtered by my publisher.)

Good news is always welcome.

One Last Thing, For Kindle Readers...

When you turn the page, Kindle will give you the opportunity to rate this book and share your thoughts on Facebook and Twitter. If you enjoyed my writings, would you please take a few seconds to let your friends know about it? Because... when they enjoy they will be grateful to you and so will I.

Thank You!

Chris Johns
chris_johns@awesomeauthors.org